GOOD OR BAD

Barbara Cartland

Barbara Cartland Ebooks Ltd

This edition © 2021

Copyright Cartland Promotions 1993

ISBNs

9781788674720 EPUB

9781788674737 PAPERBACK

Book design by M-Y Books
m-ybooks.co.uk

THE BARBARA CARTLAND ETERNAL COLLECTION

The Barbara Cartland Eternal Collection is the unique opportunity to collect all five hundred of the timeless beautiful romantic novels written by the world's most celebrated and enduring romantic author.

Named the Eternal Collection because Barbara's inspiring stories of pure love, just the same as love itself, the books will be published on the internet at the rate of four titles per month until all five hundred are available.

The Eternal Collection, classic pure romance available worldwide for all time .

THE LATE DAME BARBARA CARTLAND

Barbara Cartland, who sadly died in May 2000 at the grand age of ninety eight, remains one of the world's most famous romantic novelists. With worldwide sales of over one billion, her outstanding 723 books have been translated into thirty six different languages, to be enjoyed by readers of romance globally.

Writing her first book 'Jigsaw' at the age of 21, Barbara became an immediate bestseller. Building upon this initial success, she wrote continuously throughout her life, producing bestsellers for an astonishing 76 years. In addition to Barbara Cartland's legion of fans in the UK and across Europe, her books have always been immensely popular in the USA. In 1976 she achieved the unprecedented feat of having books at numbers 1 & 2 in the prestigious B. Dalton Bookseller bestsellers list.

Although she is often referred to as the 'Queen of Romance', Barbara Cartland also wrote several historical biographies, six autobiographies and numerous theatrical plays as well as books on life, love, health and cookery. Becoming one of

Britain's most popular media personalities and dressed in her trademark pink, Barbara spoke on radio and television about social and political issues, as well as making many public appearances.

In 1991 she became a Dame of the Order of the British Empire for her contribution to literature and her work for humanitarian and charitable causes.

Known for her glamour, style, and vitality Barbara Cartland became a legend in her own lifetime. Best remembered for her wonderful romantic novels and loved by millions of readers worldwide, her books remain treasured for their heroic heroes, plucky heroines and traditional values. But above all, it was Barbara Cartland's overriding belief in the positive power of love to help, heal and improve the quality of life for everyone that made her truly unique.

AUTHOR'S NOTE

In the reign of King George IV, the London Season started in April and ended at the beginning of June.

As the years went by, it lasted until the middle of July.

It was the dream of every *debutante* to be presented at a 'Drawing Room' in Buckingham Palace and to attend the numerous balls that were given in the large houses in Mayfair, Islington and Belgravia.

The Drawing Room was a Ceremonial Reception that was, at the beginning, always held in the Throne Room of Buckingham Palace at three o'clock precisely and there were several every year.

Later, they became an evening reception with a buffet of food and drink.

Ladies wishing to be presented could only obtain the honour through a relation or a friend who had previously been presented and with the strict approval of the Lord Chamberlain.

Débutantes, where possible, were presented by their mothers.

The lady who would make the presentation had to appear with whom she presented and in addition both of them must have unblemished characters and their conduct must be above reproach.

There was no question at all of anyone who had been through a Divorce Court being accepted.

At the first Drawing Room of the Season, the whole of the *Corps Diplomatique* were in full attendance with their elaborate gold uniforms adding to the great glamour of the ladies, who had three Prince of Wales's white feathers on their heads and a train to their gowns.

Her Majesty would then go first to the Council Room, where she would greet the Royal Family.

When the members who were expected had arrived, the Queen would be warned.

CHAPTER ONE
1875

Amalita opened the letter that had come from France.

She noticed that the envelope was not addressed in her father's usual strong upright hand.

She thought just for a moment that it must have come from her stepmother.

Then she remembered that Yvette's handwriting was very different and very French.

'Who can it be from?' she wondered.

Then she told herself that she had only to look inside to find the answer.

When she had read the letter through once, she went back to the beginning.

She stared at what was written in a such a way that would have told anyone watching that she had suffered a shock.

Finally Amalita went to sit on the window seat and gazed out into the garden.

It was nearly an hour later when the door opened and her sister Carolyn came in.

She was looking exceedingly lovely with her fair hair curled round her forehead and her face a little flushed.

Her blue eyes were the colour of the sky outside and she was so beautiful that she might have come from the sky itself.

"I have had a really marvellous ride, Amalita," she said. "I went right up to the Beacon and there was not a soul in sight."

Then, as her sister did not respond to her, she walked towards her, asking,

"What is the matter? What has happened?"

"I have just had – a letter from – France," Amalita replied nervously. "Sit down, Carolyn."

"From Papa?" Carolyn enquired. "So why should that upset you?"

She sat down because her sister had told her to and she chose a chair by the window and the sunshine turned her hair to quivering gold.

"This is a letter," Amalita said very slowly, "from the Police in Nice."

"The Police?" her sister exclaimed. "What can Papa have been up to?"

Amalita drew in her breath.

"Papa is – dead," she told her, "and so is – Yvette."

Her sister just stared at her.

After a moment she asked,

"Did you – did you say – dead?"

"Yes. According to this letter from the Police, Papa and Yvette went sailing, which, as you know, he always loved. A sudden storm got up and his yacht collided with a – cargo boat – and it sank. Their bodies were recovered, but they were already drowned."

Amalita's voice sounded so very strange, as if it was extremely difficult for her to utter the words.

Carolyn put her hands up to her eyes.

"Oh, poor Papa! How could he have gone so far away from us?"

"I find it just impossible to believe," Amalita said, "You can read the letter for yourself. It is in French."

"You know very well that my French is not as good as yours," Carolyn objected. "Tell me what it says."

"Just as I told you," Amalita replied. "Papa and Yvette went sailing. They were both drowned and the Police said it took them some time to find out who Papa was and whom they could contact."

She looked down at the letter again before she went on,

"In fact it was only when they found our letter to him that they were aware of his address."

"So they wrote to you," Carolyn said. "When did it all happen?"

"I can hardly believe it true, but it was nearly a month ago," her sister answered.

"How can they have taken so long?" Carolyn asked.

For a moment Amalita did not reply.

Then after a moment she said,

"It seems terrible to think we were enjoying ourselves and not worrying a bit about Papa and all the time he was dead."

There was another silence before Carolyn remarked,

"He did not – worry very much about – us after he – married Yvette."

Now there was a distinct bitterness in her tone, which her sister did not miss.

She jumped up from the chair and moved to put her arms around Amalita.

"I know how upset you must be," she said, "because you loved Papa and he meant so much to you. But you know, if you are truthful, that we had lost him after Mama died and he married that Frenchwoman."

Amalita drew in a deep breath.

"You are right," she agreed. "'That Frenchwoman' as you call her, changed him completely. I gather from this letter that he was not staying in Nice under his own name, which means that he did not wish to meet any of his old friends."

"How could she have a hold over him so – quickly?" Carolyn asked in bewilderment.

Her sister did not reply.

Two years older than Carolyn, she was aware that Yvette, whom her father had met in Paris, had swept him off his feet.

He had gone to Paris because he was so desperately unhappy after his wife's death and he found their home intolerable to live in.

"I see your mother in every room," he had muttered to his older daughter. "I find myself calling for her as I come in through the front door and I just cannot sleep at night because she is not beside me.

Before he could say the next words, Amalita knew what they would be.

"I must go away," Sir Frederick Maulpin said. "I must try and get control of myself, but I cannot stay here and go mad."

There was an agony as he spoke that told his daughter he was speaking the truth.

"You are so right. Papa," she said gently. "You should go away and I know when you come back that things will seem different."

She helped him to pack up his boxes and Sir Frederick had left the next day.

He did not take his valet with him and Amalita knew that it was because he was trying hard to forget everything that his home had meant to him for twenty-one years.

Because she was older than her sister and so closer to their father, he had told her that he had been a somewhat raffish young man in his youth.

She guessed that he had had very many love affairs, enjoyed himself in London and travelled on the Continent whenever he felt like it.

He was indeed well off.

He could afford all the perquisites for the pleasure of a handsome, hearty young man who had nothing better to do than to enjoy himself.

He had a stable full of fine horses and he hunted with two of the best packs in the County of Leicestershire.

He had two or three horses that had won several minor races.

He played polo and belonged to two of the smartest Gentleman's Clubs in St. James's, White's and Boodles.

Amalita knew without his telling her that he had been on the lists as a most eligible bachelor of every important hostess in London.

When he went to stay in France or any other country in Europe, he was able to stay at the British Embassy.

He was the guest of noble families in many countries he visited.

He was the eighth Baronet and the family was known as one of the oldest and most respected in England.

Queen Victoria frequently invited him to luncheon and dinner parties at Windsor Castle.

Then, so unexpectedly that it surprised even him, he fell head-over-heels in love.

Amalita knew only too well that her mother had been overwhelmingly beautiful, but not of great social standing.

Her father was a gentleman and a Country Squire.

He had, however, never aspired to shine brightly in the smartest Society in which he moved.

Having lost his heart, his character and his personality changed.

He bought a pretty black and white Medieval house in Worcestershire with a large estate and settled down there with the woman he loved.

He forgot the friends who had been so close to him in London.

The only disappointment in all the years that followed was that he did not have a son.

His first-born was a daughter who resembled him.

He christened her "Amalita" because he thought that she looked like a Greek Goddess.

She was quite different from her mother in that she had dark hair with strange lights in it and her eyes were the green-grey of the sea.

"She is just so lovely," Sir Frederick declared, "that I really believe, my darling, that she is a gift from God."

Their second daughter, Carolyn, who was born two years later, closely resembled Elizabeth Maulpin.

She also had a very sweet and gentle character, which made everyone she met love her as they loved her mother.

Amalita could be fiery and forceful, so like her father. She also had his imagination and his acute intelligence.

It amazed him, having all these fine attributes, that he should be content with one woman in the country.

In some extraordinary way it was as if they were the complete complement of each other.

It was her father who had told Amalita about what the Greeks believed in.

When man was first created, he was alone in the world and wanted a companion. So the Gods cut him in half.

Always for the rest of his existence he looked for the woman who was the other half of himself so that he would become whole again.

That was certainly what her father and mother were, Amalita felt and she could never recall them quarrelling or even arguing with each other.

Arguing was what she enjoyed when she grew older and her father found it most amusing that she had the same sharp brain that he had.

She also had an intuition that made them duel often with each other in words.

"When you do marry, my darling," he had said to her once, "I hope you will find a man who will not only adore you but also stimulate your mind in the same way that you stimulate mine."

Just a year ago, however, disaster had struck them.

It was an extremely cold winter.

However strong the fires blazed away in the house and timber was cut up to provide warmth, Elizabeth Maulpin succumbed to the freezing atmosphere and retired to bed.

It was unlike her not to be at her husband's side.

Sir Frederick, for the very first time, seemed to be at a loose end.

So it was Amalita who had ridden out with him at the strangest hours just because he could not think of anything else to do.

"Mama will soon be better, Papa," she would say to cheer him up.

Lying in the comfortable bed with its silk curtains and gold corola above it, Elizabeth Maulpin seemed to shrink away day by day.

Finally one sunny morning when her husband woke, he found her dead beside him.

His two daughters found it as difficult to believe as he did.

He was at once in such a frantic state of despair that they spent every moment of their time trying to comfort him.

"We must not leave him alone," Amalita had said to Carolyn.

They took it in turns always to be at his side.

When the funeral was over and he could no longer see the wife he had adored, he announced that he must go away.

"I shall go to Paris," he replied when Amalita asked him where he would go.

He had been away for many months.

Although the girls wrote long letters to him almost daily, they received only a few scanty replies from him.

Then, after a long empty interval, a letter arrived just as they were returning from riding.

"A letter from Papa!" Amalita exclaimed as she came into the hall. "Thank Goodness. I was just wondering what could have happened to him."

"Maybe he is coming back home at last," Carolyn said cheerfully.

Amalita opened the letter and began to read what her father had written.

"Read me the letter to me," Carolyn begged, coming up beside her.

As Amalita was silent, Carolyn took the letter from her and read it.

Then she exclaimed,

"I don't believe it! How could Papa be in love with anyone so – soon after Mama – ?"

Her voice broke and she burst into tears.

"Papa has – forgotten – Mama," she sobbed.

Amalita put her arms around her.

"He could never forget Mama" she said. "It is just that he cannot bear to be alone."

Her father returned a month later.

He brought with him his new wife, and the two girls stared at her feeling that they must be dreaming.

Yvette was in every way a complete contrast to their mother.

For one thing she was French.

Although Amalita did not say so, she was sure that she was a *Bourgeoise*.

She was certainly not an aristocrat by any means.

She did have, however, all the enticement, allure and charm for which Frenchwomen are renowned.

She walked into the house wearing high-heeled shoes and dressed in a fashion Amalita had never seen before.

It was so obvious that her father found her irresistible as he could not take his eyes from her.

She flirted with him in a way that kept the two girls gazing at her in astonishment.

She was witty and amusing and she looked at him in a way that brought the fire into his eyes.

Amalita was old enough to understand why her father could forget everything he had lost.

In fact he was no longer the father she knew, the man she had adored ever since he had first lifted her out of the cradle.

For their father's sake, Amalita and Carolyn tried to understand and to like their stepmother. But it was quite obvious that Yvette had no use for them.

She was concerned with one thing only and that was keeping their father madly and wildly in love with her.

She accepted the presents he bought for her to express his affection.

Furs, jewels, clothes of every description came down from London day after day.

Always she wanted more and still more.

Sir Frederick produced all his gifts as if he was paying her for the pleasure she gave him.

That, Amalita thought secretly when she was alone at night, was the truth.

It was very obvious that Sir Frederick did not want his friends or neighbours to meet Yvette.

That was the reason why when he returned to England he had not taken her to London.

When he came to the country, he made every excuse not to invite any of the friends who lived near them to a meal.

He refused every invitation as soon as it arrived.

It was obvious after two of three weeks that Yvette was growing restless.

"Let's go to London, *mon chéri*," Amalita heard her say to her father.

"Why London?" Sir Frederick enquired.

"It is dull here, except, of course, that I am so happy with you," Yvette replied caressingly. "But I want to go to the theatre, I want to dance with you and feel you hold me close in your arms."

"I can do that without having to dance," Sir Frederick told her.

"But I want the music. It is so romantic and, when I am with you, I feel very, very romantic, *mon brave*."

There was a note in her voice, Amalita just knew, that made Sir Frederick reach out for her.

Because it made her embarrassed when she saw her father kissing the Frenchwoman, she left the room.

But she had not forgotten what had been said.

It was therefore no surprise when only a week later her father declared that they were going back to France.

It was November and, to his daughters' surprise, he had made no effort to join any of the shooting parties to which he was invited, as he had every year previously.

He had not even hunted as he always had enjoyed.

Nor had he taken part in the Steeplechases in which he had invariably been the winner.

He just stayed at home with Yvette. More often than not they remained in their bedroom for most of the day.

The idea that they were to go to France made Yvette more animated than ever.

She talked very quickly, using her hands to express what she was saying.

She flattered Sir Frederick in such a manner that made Amalita feel embarrassed.

Before they left she said to her father,

"You have not forgotten, I hope, Papa, that Mama had plans for Carolyn to 'come out' next Season in London?"

She knew that her father had forgotten and she went on,

"I missed my debut because, if you will remember it, Grandmama died and we were in mourning. But Mama promised that we would go

~15~

to London next April and we would both be presented to the Queen."

"Yes, yes, of course, I do remember it," Sir Frederick replied impatiently, "and I promise you shall have a ball in London and also one here when we return."

"You will be back with us for Christmas?" Amalita asked him. "Then, when the Festivities are over, you can write to your friends, telling them that we are coming to London. I know that you and Mama made a list."

"Of course, of course," Sir Frederick agreed. "We will talk about it then. Just look after everything while I am away and see that the horses are well exercised."

"I will," Amalita promised, "but we shall miss you, Papa."

She spoke wistfully.

It had been a terrible year without her mother.

Now, when they had only just been able to put aside the black gowns that she and Carolyn hated, her father was going away again.

"You will be back for Christmas?" she asked again.

Even as she spoke, she had the strange feeling that he was slipping, like quicksand, through her fingers.

She could not hold on to him.

"Yes – yes, of course," Sir Fredrick said hastily. "It is just that your stepmother dislikes the cold and she will find it warmer in Paris."

The girls spent Christmas alone.

Presents arrived, which they thought were very pretty and had obviously been extremely expensive.

But it was certainly not the same as having their father with them.

'He will be back by January' Amalita told herself.

Then they learnt that he had gone to Nice.

From there he wrote to them saying,

"It will be warmer in the South and I have rented a villa outside Nice, which has a fine view overlooking the sea and quite a large garden."

Because he had described it, Amalita thought that he was going to invite them to join him.

But there was no mention of it and he merely urged them again to exercise the horses.

Finally she wrote to him, begging him to come back and reminding him that it would soon be April.

"You must, Papa, write to your friends in London," she reminded him.

She was so certain that he would return as soon as he received her letter that she started buying new dresses for herself and Carolyn.

"All your best gowns must come from Bond Street," she said. "There are only one or two shops in Worcester that seem to have up to date models and we cannot arrive looking like country bumpkins!"

Carolyn laughed.

"You could never look like one, darling Amalita and I am sure that all the smart people in London will admire your green eyes and your dark hair."

Amalita would have been very stupid, which she was not, if she had not realised that she was very striking to look at.

Carolyn was as beautiful as her mother had been.

Amalita was quite certain that the Social world would be bowled over by her.

Time was getting on and she was growing more and more worried when there was no sign of her father.

'He must arrive soon,' she had kept telling herself.

Now, having received the tragic news of his death as she held Carolyn against her, she felt the tears in her own eyes.

She knew that she had not only lost her father, but he had somehow taken the future away with him.

'What are we to do?' she wondered frantically.

Tea was announced by an old servant. He had been with them ever since her father and mother had come to live in Worcestershire.

Because she could not bear to say the words, Amalita found it impossible to tell him that her father was dead.

Instead they went into the drawing room.

She sat down on the large sofa where her mother had always sat to pour out the tea.

It had been served in the Georgian silver teapot that had belonged to their great-grandmother.

When they were at last alone, Carolyn stammered in a choked voice,

"W-what are we – going to do?"

"There is nothing we can do," Amalita said. "It says in the letter that Papa and our stepmother are buried in the Catholic Churchyard in Nice. The Police have asked what we would like put on the tombstone – if we are prepared to pay for one – and, of course, I must reply to them."

Carolyn did not say anything and after a short moment Amalita said,

"I realise from this letter that Papa was not using his title. He did not wish to see any friends who were staying in Nice."

"I believe that he was – ashamed of – the woman he married," Carolyn suggested.

This was something that Amalita had known for quite some time.

She had, however, thought it best not to express it in words.

She had also been aware that Yvette was not the sort of woman her mother would have invited to the house at any time.

From some of the things Yvette had said inadvertently Amalita was sure she had a somewhat strange past before she had married their father.

"I would suppose," Carolyn said in a doleful voice, "we cannot – now go to – London and all those – pretty gowns that we bought – will be wasted."

She gave a little sob before she added,

"I was so – looking forward to – attending balls and – meeting new people. There is – no one round here – who is – interested in us."

Amalita knew that this was true.

Their neighbours were all old and their children were already married and had left Worcestershire.

Two of the young men the girls had known since they were small had joined the Army and were posted abroad.

Another was perpetually at sea as he was a sailor.

Carolyn was right.

There was in reality no one for them to know of any interest or standing in the County.

And yet they had been very happy while their father and mother were alive.

"I am nearly eighteen," Carolyn was saying, "and it is not fair that I should just stay here with nothing to do until I am as old as you."

She saw the expression on Amalita's face and jumped up and put her arms round her neck.

"That was unkind of me," she said. "I know how you could not go to London as Grandmama had died and then Mama left us. But I really did think that Papa would come home. I suppose that horrid Yvette would not let him."

Amalita held her sister closer and she said,

"I know what you are feeling now. It is what I have been feeling too for a long time."

"What can – we do about – it?" Carolyn asked with a little sob.

~21~

"We will do something," Amalita replied firmly and now her voice sounded very much like her father's.

Unexpectedly she gave a cry.

"What is it?" Carolyn asked.

She did not really expect an answer, but Amalita said slowly,

"I have an – idea and it is – something that seems – impossible, but we will – yes – we will do it!"

Carolyn moved away from her arms.

"Tell me your idea," she pleaded.

Amalita walked across the room to the window.

She stood gazing with unseeing eyes at the sunshine flooding the garden.

Carolyn watched her.

She was trying not to be too optimistic that her sister had found a good solution to the prospect of their sitting dismally at home alone.

At the same time Amalita had always been original ever since they were children.

It was Amalita who thought of the games they would play, Amalita who climbed trees and swam in the lake.

It was Amalita who made them dress up to look like ghosts and frighten the old servants, Amalita who had got them both up on the roof of the old barn.

There they had to sit until someone came to rescue them because they could not find a way down.

Watching her sister now, Carolyn thought how lovely Amalita was in her own way.

She was indeed so unlike their mother, but there was a distinct look of her father.

Where he had been outstandingly handsome, she was beautiful.

Her sister turned round.

"I will tell you what we are going to do, Carolyn," she said. "You shall not be robbed of your debut. It was what Mama wanted for you and it is what you will have. We are going to London!"

Carolyn clasped her hands together.

"It sounds wonderful. But how can we? How can I be presented to the Queen without Mama? She always said that Papa's relations were either dead or too old and what was left of her family had always lived in the dark wilds of Northumberland."

"I know all that," Amalita said. "But, if you wish to be presented, so you must have somebody grand to take you to Buckingham Palace."

"But – who? Who can do – that?" Carolyn asked.

The excitement that there had been in her eyes for a moment or two was fading away.

She felt she knew the end of the story and that what Amalita was planning for her was just fantasy.

"We will most surely go to London," Amalita insisted slowly, "and you will be chaperoned both at the balls you will attend and at Buckingham Palace."

"By whom?" Carolyn asked. "You yourself know that there is nobody."

"*I* will be your chaperone!" Amalita announced.

Carolyn stared at her before she countered,

"You are teasing me, which only makes things worse. I may not be as clever as you, but I am well aware that a chaperone cannot be an unmarried girl. I cannot imagine you have a husband hidden away in one of the outhouses!"

She spoke with a little sting in her voice as she felt so disappointed.

Just for a moment she had hoped that because Amalita was so clever, she had solved the problem.

Then Amalita said,

"I don't intend to chaperone you as an unmarried girl but as Lady Maulpin."

Carolyn stared at her.

"Lady Maulpin? But you cannot pretend to be Mama! Even the most stupid man who ever lived – and certainly not the Dowagers who sit round the dance floors – could mistake you for Mama."

"I would not pretend to be Mama," Amalita said, "but your stepmother!"

Carolyn gasped.

"You will – pretend – to be – Yvette?"

Amalita shook her head violently.

"Certainly not! Yvette was a common and very vulgar Frenchwoman. Although she married Papa, fortunately few people in England will have seen her – and nobody in London."

Carolyn's eyes seemed to fill her whole face.

"What – are you – saying? I just don't understand. Explain it to – me."

"I am working it out in my mind," Amalita answered. "Papa was indeed married to Yvette, but they were buried as *'Monsieur et Madame Maupin'*, which, if you look at the letter, the Police have spelt wrongly. That is the name I shall order to be put on the tombstone."

She paused and then she went on,

"There is no reason for anyone to know that Papa and our stepmother have only recently been

~25~

drowned and they will certainly not go looking for their tombstone."

"And – what does that – mean?" Carolyn asked in bewilderment.

"It means that as far as we are both concerned, Papa married her nine months ago. He died almost immediately after the Wedding was over and Lady Maulpin has been in mourning. She is doing her duty in bringing to London Sir Frederick's daughter, Carolyn, who has just reached the age of eighteen."

Carolyn was listening as if she could hardly believe what she was hearing.

Then she said almost in a whisper,

"Do – you think – anyone will – believe that?"

"Why should they question it?" Amalita asked. "We have been buried alive here. No one has been interested in us since Mama died and Papa has been away. When he did come back, no one except the servants will recall having seen him."

"Don't you – think that they might – talk?" Carolyn questioned.

"In London?"

"I see – what you – mean, but, Amalita, you don't look old enough."

"Nor did Yvette! She admitted to being twenty-six, although I thought her older but I could not prove it."

She walked across the room and back again as if it was impossible to keep still.

"I will find some clothes that will make me look like a married woman and I will do my hair the way Mama used to do hers. I will also use just a little of the cosmetics that Yvette left behind."

"You never told me she had left anything behind," Carolyn exclaimed.

"Well, she did," Amalita replied, "but I did not think it of any importance. And there are the two gowns Papa bought for her that she always hated. She said they were too severe, but Papa bought them from a very expensive shop."

She gave a wry smile as she added,

"I think that he was trying to tone her down a little. Perhaps he even thought that if she wore them he could introduce her to some of his friends. But, when the gowns arrived, she put them on one side and said to me. 'I have no intention of wearing those dingy ladylike clothes that will make me look like a middle-aged frump'."

"You did not tell me she said that," Carolyn replied somewhat accusingly.

"Why should I? I thought at the time how vulgar her behaviour was."

"I just cannot think what Papa saw in her," Carolyn murmured.

Amalita was recalling how her father had come into the room at that moment.

Yvette had sprung up and run from the dressing table into his arms.

"*Merci, chéri! Je t'adore!*" she cooed. "I am thrilled with the presents you have given me!"

She had been wearing very little.

Only her topless stays that were tightly laced to keep in her waist and a transparent petticoat trimmed with real lace.

She put her arms around Sir Frederick and pulled his head down to hers. She kissed him and went on kissing him as Amalita slipped from the room.

She had known then that it would be just impossible for her father ever to escape from Yvette.

Now, as she remembered these two gowns, she knew that they were exactly what she wanted at least until she could buy some in London.

"I-I just don't think we can do it – " Carolyn was saying. "I am – sure we – will be discovered."

"You are going to have your Season in London if we die in the attempt," Amalita declared. "And if we are very lucky, you will find a husband who will love you and you will love him."

She could see her sister looking at her wide-eyed and she explained,

"That is the whole idea of the Season. You will have a lot of competition in finding the right man, but I will back you one hundred percent as a winner in the Matrimonial Stakes!"

CHAPTER TWO

When Carolyn went up to change her clothes, Amalita sat down at her father's desk.

She found the address book in which he had kept the names and addresses of all his old friends, the people with whom he had associated with before his first marriage.

Among them she found the name of the Marquis of Garlestone whom he had always stayed with on the few occasions when he visited London.

They had been great friends and Amalita remembered him saying so often.

Now in her elegant handwriting she wrote,

"My Lord,

My late husband, Sir Frederick Maulpin, often used to speak of you and your kindness to him when he was a young man and later when he stayed with you sometimes after he was married.

Now that I am out of mourning, I feel it is my duty to bring my stepdaughter to London for the Season.

She will be eighteen in a month's time and is as beautiful as her mother was.

Could your Lordship be exceedingly kind and

allow us to stay with you for two or three days while we look for a suitable house in which to entertain? I know it will not be easy to find one, but I am eager to do the best I can for Carolyn.

She must be presented at Buckingham Palace and as well attend the balls that her father and mother always wished her to enjoy.

Please, please, help me and allow us to stay with you or else perhaps your Lordship could recommend a respectable hotel.
I remain,
Yours most sincerely,

Anna Maulpin."

She hated having to change her Christian name. But it was too unusual for it not to be remembered.

Carolyn had called her "Am am" when she was a baby so it was easy for her to remember that she was now called "Anna".

She remembered her father telling her once that good agents in disguise "thought" themselves into the character and personality of whoever they were pretending to be.

"It is not only what you say and do when you are in disguise," Sir Frederick had advised. "It is also what you think. That is what I am told by a friend of mine, who has undertaken many dangerous missions in enemy territory."

The great City of London was "enemy territory" as far as she was concerned, Amalita decided.

She knew that she would have to be very careful not to be discovered and denounced as an imposter.

It would most certainly be a disaster not only for her but even more for Carolyn.

She loved her younger sister and she thought rather pathetically that Carolyn was the only one now left of her family.

Once they had been so complete, just the four of them, father, mother and the two girls.

Now, as she was the elder, she had to take command.

She could only pray and pray that she would not make a mess of it.

When she had finished the letter, she then put it into an envelope and addressed it to the Marquis of Garlestone.

She then looked through her father's address book to see who else she might be able to contact.

Fortunately her mother had been most methodical in everything that she undertook.

She had put a red spot next to the people Sir Frederick intended to contact

His friends all had distinguished names and important titles and Amalita felt a little shiver go through her in case they refused to help, thinking that she would be a person like Yvette.

Then she told herself proudly that she was her father's daughter.

From all that her mother had told her, he had been a most welcome guest in every house he had visited.

"When I first married your father," Elizabeth Maulpin said, "he had so many invitations that I used to tease him about them."

"And did you go to the parties too, Mama?" Amalita asked.

"I went to them when we were engaged and just after we were married," her mother replied, "but your father then decided that they bored him."

"Bored him, Mama?" Amalita exclaimed.

Her mother laughed.

"I think, my dearest, if I am honest, it was not because your father disliked the people and the parties that he had enjoyed so much as a bachelor but because I received too many compliments."

"I am not surprised, Mama. You must have been very beautiful."

"People were very kind with the flattering things they said," Elizabeth Maulpin replied, "but your father wanted me to himself."

It was what Sir Frederick had wanted right up until the day his wife died.

Amalita thought that it very romantic. They meant so much to each other that nothing and nobody else was of any importance.

But it was going to make it difficult now for Carolyn and herself.

She was not even certain if her father's friends were still alive. And, if they were, whether they still had the warm affection for him that they had felt in the past.

She looked at their names on the pages.

Then she told herself that the sensible thing to do was to wait until she reached London.

Then she would ask the Marquis about those whose names were marked in the address book.

'First things first,' she told herself firmly.

Then she wondered frantically what she would do if the Marquis was no longer alive.

Or if he wrote back to say that it was not convenient to have them to stay with him.

Having raised Carolyn's hopes, she knew it would be sheer cruelty to dash them now.

She sent up a fervent prayer that things would work out as she hoped.

'Help me, Papa, you must help me now,' she said in her heart.

A wave of misery swept over her, knowing that she would never see him again.

They had been very close.

Although he had adored his lovely wife to distraction, Amalita knew that she held a very significant place in his affections.

That was, of course, until Yvette came along.

He had been so besotted with her that he did not want to remember his life as it had been before her mother died.

Because Amalita was intelligent and innocent though she was of the world outside of Worcestershire, she could understand why her father had re-married.

She had read enough books to know that when men were in despair or bereaved, they drank too much to forget their sorrow.

Her father had always been abstemious and had drunk very little.

So instead, crazy though it did seem, he had married Yvette.

She had kept him from feeling so alone and bereft and with her he had been able to forget his overwhelming love for his wife. It had filled his life so completely that he had had no interests apart from her.

The thought of Yvette made Amalita shudder.

She could see her so clearly in the flamboyant clothes that she wore, which her mother would have considered vulgar.

She could now see her painted face and the way that she enticed her father with every word that she said and every movement she made.

Amalita sighed.

She decided that it was best not to dwell too much on the past.

She had to concentrate on Carolyn and her future.

She very much hoped that her sister would meet with someone of high standing who would fall in love with her.

She would not then have to return, when the Season was over, to the loneliness of their empty house.

'I don't know if we will have enough money to stay in London for very long,' she admitted to herself, 'especially if we have to rent a house.'

After her mother's death, when her beloved father had first gone abroad, he had said to her,

"You are old enough now, my dearest, for me to give you Power of Attorney while I am away."

Amalita looked puzzled and her father explained,

That means that you can sign cheques at the Bank as well as any legal document appertaining to the estate that would normally require my signature."

"I hope I can manage it for you, Papa," Amalita said.

"Of course you can," her father replied. "It is not very difficult. There is enough money in the Bank and you will both be comfortable and have whatever you want while I am away."

He had not discussed the matter any further.

Amalita had indeed not found it difficult to draw out what was required for the wages and housekeeping.

At the end of the third month of her father's absence, she had to sign a lease for a new farm tenant.

Now it struck her that the Bank would not be aware that her father was dead unless she told them.

She could therefore go on drawing what money she required without there being any difficulty about it.

She thought about writing to the Bank and asking how much there was left in her father's account.

Then she recalled that by the time they had replied, she and Carolyn might have left for London.

'I will leave it for the moment,' she thought. 'I don't want them asking questions as to when I think Papa will be returning.'

Later that evening she went to the room that Yvette had occupied during her stay in the house.

It was on her father's insistence that she had not been given the room that had always been his wife's.

It had pleased Amalita greatly to realise that, while he was infatuated with Yvette, her mother still had a special place in his heart that he would not despoil.

Instead, Yvette had used the bedroom that was across the corridor.

It was not next to his as her mother's had been.

Being the best spare room, it was most attractively decorated as indeed were all the rooms in the house.

It had been cleaned and tidied after Yvette had left.

Even so, as Amalita went into the room she could at once smell the strong exotic French perfume that Yvette had always used. It was so overpowering that she opened the window.

Then she went to the wardrobe to see what Yvette had left behind.

She knew that there would be the two gowns that Sir Frederick had bought for her in London but she had then refused to wear them.

As Amalita looked at them she thought that they were exactly what she needed at the moment.

One was dark blue and smart with an elegant bustle and the other was the colour of Parma violets and had a bustle made of little frills of a deeper purple.

'I will certainly look older in these two,' Amalita told herself.

Then she saw there were two or three other gowns hanging up.

They were very different and she shrank away from them as if they were unclean.

They were in bright brilliant colours and cut very low over the breast and their bustles were exaggeratedly large.

Amalita took out from the wardrobe the two gowns that her father had bought and laid them on the bed.

She then went to the dressing table.

Opening one of the drawers she found the cosmetics that she knew Yvette had left behind.

When the housemaid had gone to clean the room, she had enquired,

"Should I throw these things away, Miss Amalita?"

She was clearly shocked at the thought of any woman painting her face.

"No, of course not," Amalita replied. "I am sure that her Ladyship will expect to find them where she left them when she comes back to Worcestershire."

The housemaid, who had been with them for several years, sniffed her disapproval. But she did not say what was in her thoughts.

Now Amalita looked at the powder and a small pot of rouge and another box that contained mascara.

She had thought Yvette's eyelashes were unnaturally dark and at least that was something she would not need.

She had inherited her father's dark hair and as well his long dark eyelashes.

When she looked at herself in the mirror, she thought that they framed her green eyes very effectively.

Because she was dark, whilst Carolyn was very fair, she automatically looked older than she was.

What she did not realise was that there was something not exactly young but spiritual about her face and eyes.

It was something that no one could have found about Yvette.

Carrying the cosmetics and the gowns, Amalita went to her own bedroom.

Once there, she inspected her own wardrobe.

She thought that there was little she could wear that did not make her look her right age and certainly not five years older.

Then, with what was a real effort, she went into her mother's room.

No one had slept in it.

Because it was too painful to do, neither Amalita nor Carolyn had gone into the bedroom since her mother had passed away

It was cleaned every week and the door would be left open while the housemaids were working there.

But the two girls hurried past, knowing it made them want to cry to think that Elizabeth Maulpin was not in the big canopied bed.

She had looked so lovely even when she was ill.

She would smile and hold out her arms as soon as she saw them.

Now in the room, Amalita closed the door and then she said in a low voice,

"You will – have to – help me, Mama. I am doing – this for Carolyn and I am – sure you will – understand that I must – not make any mistakes."

As she spoke, the tears came into her eyes.

Then, as she wiped them away, the last dying glimmer of the sun came through the windows.

It glittered on the mirrors, the pictures and the large collection of ornaments that her mother had collected and loved.

For a few moments Amalita could see nothing but the golden glory of it.

Then she told herself that it was the answer that she had sought.

She was doing the right thing and her mother would most certainly help her.

Quite suddenly her apprehension and her fear left her.

She was not alone and, as her mother had believed, there was no such thing as death.

She went to the wardrobe, feeling that it was foolish that she had not come into the room before.

Instead of feeling unhappy, as she thought that she would be, she had felt that her mother was there with her.

It was almost as if she could hear her talking to her in her soft gentle voice.

Amalita looked through her mother's gowns.

Some of them, she realised, were now completely out of fashion.

The crinoline had been replaced by the bustle, which had been acclaimed in Paris and then quickly adopted in London.

So Amalita had not needed to take a look at Yvette's over-exaggerated bustles to know what was smart in the fashionable world.

Her mother had always taken *The Ladies Journal* and because Amalita had not bothered to cancel the magazine, it had continued to arrive. It contained many sketches and photographs of famous people that told her exactly what was correct and what was incorrect.

Her mother had bought several gowns from the best shop in Worcester and the village seamstress was quite an expert with her needle.

Lady Maulpin had asked her to make several dresses for Amalita and Carolyn.

As she grew older, Amalita had had some gowns from the same shop that her mother patronised.

"They are not what you should have as a *debutante*." her mother said, "and it is so very depressing, dearest, that instead of going to London, we have to be in mourning for Grandmama. But we will certainly go later."

That was what had been intended until her mother fell ill.

Amalita had disliked the black gowns she had been forced to wear for the first two or three months after her grandmother's death.

She had therefore not bothered as to whether they had a bustle or not.

When she was then in half-mourning, her gowns were mostly white but with a black sash.

Her mother, however, had bought some pretty black gowns for herself, which were trimmed with white.

As Amalita took them from the wardrobe, she thought that they would certainly suit her as a widow, even though she had no intention of being dressed only in black.

Her mother's gowns fitted her while for Carolyn they would have been too long.

'I will spend everything that we can afford in making Carolyn look beautiful,' Amalita decided.

In the closet there was a nice evening cloak lined with ermine and several other capes and wraps that were most definitely designed for an older woman.

Amalita took them to her bedroom and packed them herself.

She had no wish for the servants to think it odd that she was taking her mother's clothes with her to London.

She next collected all her mother's jewellery from the safe where it was kept.

There was not a great deal of it. What there was had been given to Elizabeth Maulpin by her mother, who had exceedingly good taste.

As Amalita packed these, she remembered that there was another safe in her father's bedroom.

There she found a tiara and a necklace of diamonds and pearls that Elizabeth Maulpin had never worn.

They belonged to Sir Frederick's grandmother and her mother had said that they were too heavy for her.

Amalita packed them all safely into her trunk.

She then wondered if by chance the Marquis would not have them, where could they possibly go.

She thought it could be dangerous to take things that were so valuable to a hotel.

'I will have to wait and see what he says,' she mused. 'It is no use being impatient when he may not even be in London.'

It was difficult for the next two days not to run into the hall every time she heard the postman's knock.

She invariably felt depressed when there was no letter for her.

Carolyn had now become enthusiastic about the idea of going to London and could talk of nothing else.

"How many balls do you think I might be invited to, Amalita?" she asked.

And then less optimistically,

"Supposing when I go to a ball and then nobody asks me to dance? That would be terribly embarrassing."

Amalita looked at her sister with her golden hair and blue eyes.

She reflected that it would be impossible for any man who saw her not to wish to make her acquaintance.

"You will be a great success in London, Carolyn," she said aloud. "But you will have to remember to call me 'Stepmama' and not 'Amalita'."

"I am sure I shall – forget," Carolyn confessed.

"Well, as I am a young stepmother, I don't suppose it would matter if you did use my Christian name," Amalita said. "But it is very important that people should not have any idea that I am not a widow or your stepmother and therefore the right person to chaperone you."

"It is like playing *Charades*," Carolyn laughed, "and what we really have to do is not to forget our lines."

"That certainly is very important," Amalita replied.

*

It was three days later when the postman brought the letter that Amalita had been waiting for.

She thought that three days had never taken so long to pass.

She had lain awake at night trying to plan what to do for Carolyn if the Marquis did refuse to have them as his guests.

~47~

The letter had finally arrived and a footman brought it into the drawing room where Amalita was sitting.

She had been looking for the thousandth time at her father's address book.

"Here be a letter that's addressed to Lady Maulpin, Miss Amalita," the maid said.

Amalita jumped up from the sofa.

"A letter?" she exclaimed as though she had not been expecting one.

She picked it up and even before she saw the most impressive crest on the back of the envelope, she knew that it was from the Marquis.

She went to the window and told herself that it was ridiculous, but her hands were trembling.

Forcing herself to do it neatly, she opened the letter.

The handwriting was very easy to read, she thought, but somewhat unsteady, as if written by an elderly man.

She read,

"Dear Lady Maulpin,
It was a great surprise to me and also a shock to learn that my dear friend Frederick had died without my being aware of it. I certainly missed the announcement of it in the newspapers,

otherwise I would have written a letter of condolence immediately.

I also had no idea that his wife had died and that he had remarried.

In view of our long friendship, it would give me great pleasure to entertain you here at my house in Park Lane, where I shall be staying during the summer months. If you will let me know when you and your stepdaughter will be arriving, I will send a carriage to meet you at the Station.

Your husband was certainly one of my oldest and dearest friends and I find it hard to believe that I shall never see him again,
Yours sincerely,

Garlestone."

Amalita read the letter slowly to the end and then she gave a whoop of joy.

"I have won! *I have won!*"

The Marquis would have them and all she had to do now was to reply to the letter and take Carolyn to London as quickly as possible.

When her sister then came in from her riding, Carolyn knew before Amalita said anything what had happened.

One glance at her sister's face was enough.

"He will have us! I know the Marquis will have us," she exclaimed.

"You are very right," Amalita replied. "He has written me a charming letter inviting us both to stay at his house in Park Lane."

Carolyn next put her arms round her sister's waist and twirled her round the room.

"We are going to London," she cried out. "I will go to balls, to the theatre and will meet dashing exciting young men!"

"You will," Amalita answered her a little breathlessly. "But remember, we will have to buy some clothes – and that means Bond Street."

"Of course we will," Carolyn agreed. "I shall be the belle of the ball, fall in love with a handsome Duke and have the most marvellous Wedding anyone has ever had!"

Because it was so like the Fairytale that Amalita had been telling herself, she laughed.

"Keep your fingers crossed," she warned, "and bow to the moon – when there is one."

"Our luck has undoubtedly changed," Carolyn said, "and everything you have planned with your clever brain, Amalita, is coming true."

Amalita held a few misgivings about that, but she did not wish to spoil Carolyn's excitement.

*

Five days later they set out for London.

When they did so, Amalita felt as if they were now climbing a mountain or swimming an Ocean, rather than just prosaically taking the train to Paddington Station.

They climbed into a reserved carriage into which they were locked by the guard. This was to prevent them from being disturbed by other travellers.

Amalita listened to all her sister's excited chatter and Carolyn put a large number of questions to her that she could not answer.

"How do we get to Buckingham Palace?"

"Do you think if you just ask the Lord Chamberlain he will give you permission to present me?"

"Which do you think will be the first ball that I will be invited?"

The questions came one after the other.

Amalita was suddenly afraid that she was now living in a 'Fool's Paradise'.

Perhaps, when they did finally reach London, Carolyn would not receive any invitations.

To save time she had written to a good number of her father's friends very much the same letter she had written to the Marquis.

All she needed now, before posting them, was to find out whether they were still in existence and had not died.

As the train puffed into the Station at Paddington, she wondered if she had in fact invented the whole story.

Perhaps there was no Marquis and no one in London to welcome them.

Her fears, however, were quickly swept aside.

A footman in Livery stepped up to them, took off his hat and asked if she was Lady Maulpin.

When she said that she was, he explained,

"'Is Lordship has sent me to find you, my Lady, and the carriage be outside. I've also brought another one for you luggage."

Amalita had labelled all their luggage very carefully even though it was not necessary for her to identify it.

She saw that there was a most efficient-looking man waiting to see it brought from the guard's van.

She and Carolyn followed the footman.

At the entrance to the Station there was an extremely smart carriage drawn by two fine horses.

They were helped into it by the footman and, as they drove off, Carolyn put her hand into Amalita's and said,

"This is thrilling! Oh, dearest Amalita, how could you have been so clever as to make it all work so well for us?"

"Don't speak too soon," Amalita warned her, "and do remember, dearest, that I am your stepmother."

Carolyn looked at her sister as if for the first time.

"You do look different," she said, "I am sure that no one would guess for a single moment that you are only just twenty."

She paused before she added,

"I wish in a way that we were 'coming out' together. It would have been such fun to be ourselves as we have always been and not have to pretend."

"In which case we would have to have a chaperone," Amalita reminded her sister, "and she would doubtless be a bore, or else very critical, finding fault with everything we did."

Carolyn gave a little cry of horror.

"I would much rather have you, dearest Amalita," she said. "And now we are to meet the Marquis. Do I look all right?"

Her sister looked lovely, Amalita thought.

She had chosen for Carolyn a blue gown, which was the colour of her eyes. She was wearing a small hat that haloed her head and was trimmed with forget-me-nots.

If the Marquis was not overwhelmed by her, Amalita thought, he would have to be blind.

She herself was wearing one of her mother's black and white gowns and the pretty hat that went with it was trimmed with white quill feathers.

She had swept up her dark hair behind her ears and she was wearing a pair of her mother's pearl and diamond earrings.

She was so intent on having to look older that she did not realise that she also looked lovely and attractive.

Being rather agitated when they arrived at Paddington, she was not aware that, as she and Carolyn walked to the carriage, every man they passed stared at them.

And they had turned to look after them until they were out of sight.

It took only a short time for the horses to reach Park Lane and halfway down there was a large attractive house standing by itself.

It had a small in-and-out driveway at the front and a large garden at the back.

The carriage came to a standstill outside the heavily porticoed front door and Amalita was aware that her heart was beating much faster than usual.

This was the test.

If the Marquis thought for one moment that she was not her father's second wife, he might send them away.

Then she told herself that she was being very foolish.

Why should the Marquis doubt that she was who she said she was?

A most impressive-looking butler bowed them into the hall where there were four footmen on duty.

He led them up the stairs and opened the door to what Amalita guessed was the main reception room.

It was all very opulent with huge crystal chandeliers and several large windows opened out over the garden.

Seated before the fireplace were two gentlemen, who rose to their feet as the butler announced in a loud voice,

"Lady Maulpin and Miss Carolyn Maulpin, my Lord."

Trying to walk with dignity and with the same grace that her mother had always had, Amalita moved towards the two men.

Because she was nervous, she found it difficult to look directly at either of them.

Then she saw that a gentleman with white hair was holding out his hand.

"It is delightful to see you, Lady Maulpin," he began, "and, of course, to meet the daughter of my old friend."

He shook hands with both of them.

Then he said,

"This is my son, David."

Vaguely Amalita remembered that the Marquis had a son who was the Earl of Garle, a Courtesy title reserved for the eldest son of a Marquis.

Then she looked at him and gasped.

He was without any exception the best-looking young man she had ever seen.

Taller than his father, he had dark hair and very broad shoulders. Yet, while he was extremely good-looking, she thought that there was a cynical air about him.

It was almost as if he suspected, although, of course, it was impossible, that they were making use of his father.

"It is so very kind of you to have us to stay, my Lord," Amalita said. "I have been living quietly in the country, first with my dear husband when he was alive, then for the past year we have been in -- mourning."

She paused and her voice sounded sad as she added,

"I know no one in London and I could not think what to do except to write to you."

"I can assure you, my Lady, I am so delighted to have you here," the Marquis said, "and my son will know better than I do which balls will be the most enjoyable for your stepdaughter."

"I have never been to a ball," Carolyn said. "It will be so exciting to be able to dance at one."

She spoke eagerly and looked very pretty as she did.

Amalita knew that both men were looking at her as if they felt that she could not be real.

She began to feel the fluttering of her heart subside.

They all sat down as the footmen brought in the tea.

As they did so, Amalita was thinking that it was her father who had guided her to exactly the right place.

As they then had tea, which the Marquis asked her to pour out, he talked away, questioning her as to whom she knew.

He then asked her what arrangements she had made for presenting Carolyn to the Queen.

"I have not known what to do," Amalita said frankly, "except, my Lord, that I have a list of dear Frederick's old friends. I will write to them but, of course, they may not be in London after all these years or even alive."

"I will be able to answer that question," the Marquis said, "and what about your stepdaughter being presented?"

Amalita clasped her hands together.

"Please, please, help me," she begged. "I have no idea whom I should approach, although I suppose it is the Lord Chamberlain and he may not consider me of sufficient importance to make the presentation."

The Marquis laughed.

"If you are Frederick's wife, there is no one in The Palace who does not remember him and would not wish to help you, Lady Maulpin. Everybody in the Social world missed him when he went off to the country. I have often wondered if he missed the City lights he left behind."

"He was very very happy," Amalita replied before she could prevent herself, "or so I have always been – told, and I too was very happy with him."

"Of course you were," the Marquis agreed.

Then, unexpectedly from the far side of the fireplace, the Earl enquired,

"Where does your family come from, Lady Maulpin? And how is it possible that you yourself have not been seen in London before you married Sir Frederick?"

As he spoke, Amalita met his eyes.

Instinctively she was aware that he was dangerous.

She had the distinct feeling that he was looking at her penetratingly.

It was as if he was probing beneath the surface.

She thought it was impossible, but she was afraid that he was suspicious that she was not what she appeared to be.

'I am imagining it,' she told herself.

There was a distinct pause before she said,

"I am indeed immensely proud of my ancient family that hardly exists today. We come from the very far North of England – Northumberland, to be precise. That is why they could not help me when Carolyn wished to come to London for the Season."

"And you lived in Northumberland until you married Sir Frederick?"

'He is too inquisitive and I don't like him,' Amalita thought to herself.

She smiled before she said disarmingly,

"Carolyn and I admit that we are 'country bumpkins' and we are only afraid that when we do meet sophisticated gentlemen like you, we will make mistakes."

"I am sure that is impossible," the Marquis said before his son could reply. "And do allow me to tell you, Lady Maulpin, that neither you nor Carolyn look in the least like 'country bumpkins'."

"Thank you, my Lord," Amalita murmured.

"In fact," the Marquis went on, "I am only stating the truth when I say that I consider you both very beautiful! I only know that, if my old friend Sir Frederick was alive, he would be saying the same thing."

CHAPTER THREE

Amalita came back to the house in Park Lane flushed with excitement.

She and Carolyn had spent a very successful morning in Bond Street and they had bought some gowns that were up to date and very attractive.

They quickly tidied themselves in their rooms before luncheon.

When Amalita went down to the drawing room where the Marquis was waiting for her, she said,

"I have enjoyed myself this morning. I did not know that gowns could be so enticing. Carolyn is going to look absolutely radiant at the first party she goes to."

"I am sure of that," the Marquis replied, "and what did you buy for yourself?"

Amalita smiled at him.

"I bought two gowns, my Lord," she said, "that I hope you will think suitable."

"I am sure I shall," the Marquis said, "and I too have made a decision while you have been away."

"About what?" Amalita asked.

"I have decided to introduce you to your husband's friends," he said, "here in the house."

Amalita stared at him.

"Do you mean – a party?" she enquired.

"I mean a party and, of course, the young will want to dance. So my secretary is hiring one of the best orchestras available in London."

"How kind you are! How very kind. I never imagined – you would do – anything like that for us."

"I think it about time," he said, "that I did something not only for you and Carolyn but also for my son."

The way he spoke of the Earl made Amalita wonder if there was something strange about him that she had not noticed.

She waited, but the Marquis said no more.

At that moment Carolyn came into the drawing room.

"I hear you have been very extravagant, young lady," he said to her.

"We have bought some really lovely gowns," Carolyn answered, "and I hope you will think them very pretty."

"I am looking forward to seeing them," the Marquis smiled.

They went into the dining room, but there was no sign of the Earl and they lunched without him.

Afterwards Carolyn said that she wanted to go out into the garden.

"I do so hope you will find it attractive," the Marquis answered. "I spend a lot of money in having a garden in London and I look forward to showing you my garden at Garle Park, which, even though I say it myself, it is truly magnificent."

Thinking back to what her father had told her, Amalita said,

"I think that your country house is in the County of Hertfordshire, my Lord."

"Yes, it is and it has been in my family for over four hundred years," the Marquis told her. "Your husband used to enjoy staying there with me and, when you have seen it, I hope that you will feel the same."

This was something that Amalita really wanted to do.

She not only thanked the Marquis but then asked him to tell her about his house and its contents.

They had by now moved from the dining room back to the drawing room.

Carolyn went into the garden and, when she had gone, the Marquis said in a serious tone,

"I want to talk to you, Lady Maulpin."

Amalita sat down on the sofa, and he stood in front of the fireplace.

She thought he was thinking of how he should phrase what he wanted to say.

So there was a distinct pause before he began,

"I can see that you are very fond of your stepdaughter and she is undoubtedly exceedingly beautiful."

"That is one reason why I was so eager to bring her to London," Amalita replied.

"It would certainly be a mistake for her to be buried in the country," the Marquis remarked. "And now that she is here I have a plan that I hope you will agree to."

Amalita wondered what it could be.

She did not, however, say anything and so after a few moments the Marquis went on,

"You have met my son and, I expect, like all women, you find him very handsome?"

"Y-yes – of course," Amalita agreed.

The Earl had dined with them the night before and she had seen again that cynical and mocking expression in his eyes.

It was as if he thought that she was taking advantage of his father in some way.

He had looked very striking in his evening clothes, but she had told herself once again that she did not really like him.

It was, however, something that she could certainly not say to his father.

She merely murmured,

"I-I am sure that your son is a great – success in the Social world."

"That is true," the Marquis said. "At the same time he has a good brain and I feel that he is wasting it and just enjoying himself when there are a great many other things he could do with his life."

"What sort of things?" Amalita asked curiously.

"The Prime Minister has several times requested him to undertake missions in different parts of Europe," the Marquis answered. "To the best of my knowledge, he has accepted two and I understand was very successful."

There was a pause and after a moment he went on,

"I do not know for certain, but I rather suspect that he has refused these requests made by the Prime Minister for no other reason except that he wishes to spend his time in London."

Amalita felt a little bewildered.

"Is there any reason why he should not?" she asked.

There was silence.

She knew that the Marquis was wondering whether he should answer her question or not.

Finally he said,

"I will be truthful, Lady Maulpin, and tell you that I am in fact very worried about my son."

"For what reason?" Amalita enquired.

"The answer is the obvious one, *cherchez la femme*," the Marquis replied.

He unexpectedly walked over the room and stood for a moment at the window.

Then he walked back to the fireplace.

"I know I may be an interfering old man," he said at length, "but I cannot bear to see my son involved with a woman who is not worthy of him and whom I distrust."

This was something that Amalita had not in the least expected and she was at a loss as to how to reply to him.

"The woman in question," the Marquis went on, "is Lady Hermione Buckworth."

Amalita raised her eyebrows.

"I am rather surprised that you have not heard of her," the Marquis said.

"You forget, my Lord, I have been in the country," Amalita murmured.

"Well then, now that you are in London you will most certainly hear about Lady Hermione. She is the daughter of the Duke of Dorset and married Lord Buckworth after her first Season. He is much older than she is and stays in the country while preferring not to know anything about his wife's infidelities."

Amalita was listening intently.

This was the sort of story that her father might have told her, but it would never have come from her mother.

"Lady Hermione," the Marquis continued, "has set the whole of the Social world talking all about her outrageous behaviour and the way that she flouts convention."

He gave a sigh before he added,

"I might have easily guessed that my son would find her amusing, as do most of the men from one end of St. James's to the other."

Now there was a bitterness in his voice and Amalita said,

"You said – that Lady Hermione is – married."

"She is," the Marquis replied, "but I have been told that Lord Buckworth is extremely ill and the doctors are saying that there is little chance of saving his life."

Now Amalita began to understand why the Marquis was so perturbed.

"I am quite certain," he was saying, "because I would be very foolish to think anything else, that Lady Hermione is determined to marry my son."

"And does he want tomarry her?" Amalita asked.

"That I just don't know," the Marquis replied. "He has said a thousand times that he has no intention of marrying anybody until it becomes absolutely necessary for him to produce an heir."

He gave an audible sigh before he said,

"Ever since David left Eton he has been pursued by women, but I have never known him to be serious about any of them. The majority, of course, have been married and there was no question of it being anything else but an *affaire de coeur*."

"But surely," Amalita argued, "if Lady Hermione is as outrageous as you say, your son would not consider her a suitable wife, seeing how distinguished your family is."

There was silence before the Marquis replied,

"You may think that I am being imaginative, but if Lady Hermione becomes free, I suspect that she will find a way of trapping my son into matrimony even if he has no wish for her to be his wife."

"How can she do – that?" Amalita asked curiously.

"I just don't know," the Marquis admitted, "but she is different from most women, and beneath a very beautiful face there is, I think, the cunning of the Devil!"

This was certainly very strong language and Amalita's eyes opened wide before she asked,

"But – what can you do, my Lord?"

"What I want to do," the Marquis answered at once, "is to marry my son to your stepdaughter!"

Amalita gave a gasp.

This was something that she had never anticipated.

'It would, of course, she felt, be such a magnificent marriage socially as far as Carolyn was concerned.

Yesterday she had met the Earl.

It had never struck her that he might be the sort of man with Carolyn would dance with and enjoy herself.

He was older and obviously sophisticated.

In a way that Amalita could not explain, she was sure that he would consider her and Carolyn extremely dull and inexperienced and therefore of no interest whatsoever to him personally.

It all flashed through her mind.

Then, as she knew that the Marquis was waiting, she said,

"I am sure that if Carolyn did fall – in love with your son, it would be something that would have – pleased her father."

"I know that," the Marquis said, "and there is no one I would rather have as David's wife than Frederick's lovely daughter."

"I cannot – help but think," Amalita said tentatively, "that the Earl would think that Carolyn was too – young for him."

"My wife was only seventeen when I married her," the Marquis said, "and we were extremely happy. In fact I found her perfect in every way, except that she was able to give me only the one son when I would have liked half-a-dozen."

Amalita laughed.

"All Englishmen feel like that and my husband was always sorry that he had no sons."

"And you did not give him any?" he enquired.

There was a rather uncomfortable silence.

Amalita could not think of what to say until he went on,

"But, of course, you were married to him only for a short time. Your stepdaughter is young and I would like to have a good number of grandchildren before I die."

"Of course you would," Amalita said softly.

"What I am asking," the Marquis continued, "is that you will help me and make Carolyn realise how lucky she would be to become the Marchioness of Garlestone. I, in my turn, will do everything I can to throw the two young people together."

"Of course I will – help you," Amalita replied. "But perhaps Lady Hermione is not as dangerous as you might think, my Lord."

"Just wait until you see her," the Marquis warned her. "Then you will realise exactly what I am up against. She is a woman who creates chaos wherever she goes."

"Is she really very beautiful?" Amalita asked.

"Most men think so," the Marquis answered, "but to me she is dangerous, as dangerous as a black panther in the jungle or a cobra hiding in the undergrowth."

To Amalita it sounded exactly like a story in a book.

It could, she thought, have no relation to real life.

Yet she was intrigued and later, when they went up to dress for dinner, she said to Carolyn,

"The Marquis is so kind and I feel that we owe him a great debt of gratitude."

"It is really wonderful of him to give a party for me," Carolyn said. "I got one of the servants to show me the ballroom when I came in from the garden and it is most impressive with very fine pictures on the walls that I am sure Papa must have enjoyed when he stayed here.

"I should like you to see the pictures too," Carolyn continued, "and, my darling Amalita, you do realise that it will not only be my first ball but yours too."

Instinctively Amalita looked over her shoulder.

"Do be careful," she warned. "If anyone heard what you were saying, they would think it very strange."

Carolyn lowered her voice.

"It is very true," she said, "and please, dearest, buy a beautiful, beautiful gown so that you will look lovely too."

"I will do that," Amalita replied. "At the same time, we have to concentrate on you. I want you to be very nice to the Marquis and also to the Earl."

Carolyn laughed.

"Why are you laughing?" Amalita enquired.

"Because you can see quite clearly that the Earl does not think much of us," Carolyn answered. "I was watching him when we were talking before dinner and I am quite certain he thought that he was being very condescending in even speaking to us."

"I don't think that is true," Amalita said.

"It is," Carolyn said positively. "And even if I am nice to him, I doubt if he will even notice me."

Amalita thought that this was something she should have anticipated.

"Whatever your feelings," she said quickly, "you must try for the Marquis's sake. After all he talks as if we will be able to stay here forever and that would be much better than having a nasty cheap house of our own."

"Of course it would," Carolyn agreed, "and so I will most certainly try, but I think the Earl of Garle is a stuck-up man who dislikes girls."

When they went downstairs to dinner, Carolyn looked entrancing. She was wearing one of the new gowns that they had bought in Bond Street.

"It seems rather elaborate for a quiet dinner at home," Amalita admitted, "but it is always a good thing to try out a gown and not wear it for the first time on a very special occasion."

The gown was, of course, white, with a bustle of white lace and chiffon at the back and the bodice with its puffed sleeves emphasised Carolyn's very small waist.

Amalita could not help herself thinking that the Earl must have a heart of stone if he did not find her attractive.

They entered the drawing room where they were to meet before dinner.

To her surprise, there was not only the Marquis and his son but also several other people.

As she advanced to the fireplace, the Marquis said,

"David is entertaining some of his friends tonight. Let me introduce them to you, Lady Maulpin."

There were two women and two men who did not seem to be related and yet they were obviously on intimate terms with one another.

The women were attractive and spectacularly gowned.

The men, who were about the same age as the Earl, seemed to Amalita to have a rakish air about them.

A few minutes after Amalita and Carolyn had arrived in the room, another man arrived.

He was very obviously a relation as he addressed the Marquis as "uncle".

When he was being introduced, Amalita learned that his name was "Timothy Lambton".

He was the son of the Marquis's sister and he seemed to be younger than the other men, not exactly handsome but very pleasant-looking and he had a kind face.

He was obviously very impressed with Carolyn, who was standing beside the Earl.

Remembering her sister's instructions, she was trying to talk to him.

Although Amalita could not hear just what they were saying, she had the idea that he was not very responsive.

Champagne was being handed round by the servants, and Amalita felt that it would not be long before dinner was announced.

She wondered if the Marquis had put Carolyn beside the Earl.

Then she thought it might be too obvious, considering that they were not a large party.

She saw the Marquis glance at the clock.

Then the door opened and the butler announced,

"Lady Hermione Buckworth, my Lord."

Amalita turned round, curious to see the woman about whom she had already heard so much.

Whether the Marquis was right or not about her being evil, she was certainly beautiful.

Like herself Lady Hermione was dark and in her hair glistened a profusion of emeralds that matched her eyes.

Amalita had green eyes and they were the light and sparkling green of a mountain stream reflecting the buds of spring.

There was also a touch of gold in them that appeared to have come from the sunshine.

Lady Hermione's eyes were green, but of a different shade.

Her eyes were the deep green of the emeralds that she wore in her hair and on her neck and they slanted up just a little at the corners.

And Amalita could understand why the Marquis had compared her to a panther or a cobra.

There was something most definitely strange, exotic and perhaps also wicked about her. It made her extremely alluring as well as being overwhelming.

The bustle of her gown was of green ostrich feathers and it struck Amalita at once that it was the sort of gown that Yvette would have worn.

It was certainly cut very low at the front and revealed rather than concealed her figure.

As she moved down the room, it was with the sinuous grace of a snake.

"Forgive me if I am late," she said to the Earl, who had moved forward to greet her, "but I had a caller who would not leave me."

She looked at him from under her long eyelashes as she spoke and Amalita knew that she was trying to make him jealous.

Then swiftly she turned to the Marquis.

"How sweet of you," she said in a cooing tone, "to ask me to dinner. It is such a long time since I have dined here and you know how much I adore your wonderful house."

It was charmingly put, but rather overdone.

Amalita saw the Marquis's eyes narrow as he replied,

"I hear that your husband is not in very good health. You must be very worried about him."

"Of course I am," Lady Hermione said, "but, as you can imagine, I am not good at nursing the sick or soothing the fevered brow and my husband is content to remain in the country without me."

As if she did not wish to discuss this subject further, she turned to greet gushingly the other guests of the party.

It was obvious that the ladies were not very pleased at her arrival.

There was, however, admiration in the men's eyes, as if they found her not only amusing but irresistible.

Dinner was then announced and the Marquis offered Amalita his arm.

She was somewhat surprised.

As Lady Hermione was the daughter of a Duke, he should have taken her in.

As if he knew what she was thinking, the Marquis muttered as they walked towards the dining room,

"This is David's party tonight not mine and, following on from our conversation earlier, I should be interested to have your opinion."

Amalita gave him a little smile and there was no need to say anything more.

When they walked into the dining room, she found that she was sitting on the Marquis's right.

The Earl was at the other end of the table with Lady Hermione on one side of him and Carolyn on the other.

They made a very extraordinary contrast that Amalita almost laughed.

She knew that it was the Marquis's doing and he had a distinct twinkle in his eye as he contemplated them.

Amalita had already seen Lady Hermione looking at her, she thought, as if she was something blown in by the wind.

She ignored Carolyn completely.

It was obvious that she had no use for women.

It was only after dinner when she realised that Amalita was actually staying in the house that she paid her some attention.

"Why have I not seen you before, Lady Maulpin?" she asked. "Have you been abroad or just been vegetating in the country?"

"I have been in mourning," Amalita replied.

"But you know the Marquis. Yet I have never heard him speak of you."

"My late husband was a very great friend of our host," Amalita replied, "which is why he has been kind enough to ask Carolyn and me to stay here with him."

"That is certainly unusual," Lady Hermione remarked. "I have always understood it that he prefers to be alone, except, of course, for his son."

"Then we are very lucky," Amalita replied blandly.

She thought that there was a hint of a frown on Lady Hermione's oval forehead and a suspicious look in her green eyes.

~79~

"Are you saying that you intend to stay here for the whole of the Season?" she asked coldly.

"I hope so," Amalita answered, "but, of course, if the Marquis finds us an encumbrance, we shall have to find a house somewhere in Mayfair."

"I think it would be a far better idea," Lady Hermione answered. "The Earl has always told me what a bore it is when he comes back home to find that the house is filled with people."

"If he does feel like that," she replied, "then Carolyn and I must keep out of his way. It will not be difficult in such a big house."

It was definitely not the answer that Lady Hermione had expected and she moved away with a flounce to speak to one of the other ladies.

When they were joined by the gentlemen, the Earl said that they were all going on to another party.

"It is quite a small affair," he added.

"As it is a small party," the Marquis said, "and you are an odd number, perhaps Carolyn could join you. I am sure that you, Timothy, will look after her."

Amalita saw Carolyn's face light up.

"It would be very exciting," she told the Marquis, "but perhaps the – person giving the party will not want me."

"It is a very small party," Lady Hermione asserted in a crushing tone.

"All the better then Carolyn will not feel overpowered by it," the Marquis retorted.

He turned to his nephew.

"Now, you look after Miss Maulpin," he admonished, "and then bring her home early. I don't think you need a chaperone to accompany you just from here to Grosvenor Square."

"No, of course not, uncle," Timothy answered, "and I will most certainly take very good care of Miss Maulpin, as you suggest."

There was nothing that Amalita could say.

She was well aware of why the Marquis was adding Carolyn to the party.

It amused her to see him handing her into the same carriage with the Earl and Lady Hermione.

Timothy sat opposite her with his back to the horses.

As they then drove off, Amalita was certain that Lady Hermione was furious at her *tête-à-tête* with the Earl being interrupted.

Amalita and the Marquis went back to the drawing room. As they did so, he said,

"You did not mind my sending Carolyn with them? I just knew that it would annoy Lady

Hermione and perhaps will make David realise how very tiresome and difficult she can be."

Amalita thought it was unlikely that Lady Hermione would show that side of her character to the Earl.

She was aware that the Marquis was delighted with himself. He had struck a blow at a woman he disliked and of whom he disapproved.

She knew exactly what he was trying to do.

There was no doubt at all that Lady Hermione was an upper-class version of Yvette.

She could recall only too well how she had ensnared and captivated her father.

Anyway, even if the Marquis's dream of marrying his son to Carolyn was not to be fulfilled, at least she was in the right place and meeting the right people.

"I had never thought about it until this moment," the Marquis was saying, "but perhaps, Lady Maulpin, you too would have liked to go to the party?"

"I am perfectly content to be here with you, my Lord," Amalita replied. "It is Carolyn we have to think about and to find her plenty of partners when she goes to a ball."

"There will be plenty of partners for her right here at my ball, which I am already planning for next week."

Amalita looked at him in astonishment.

"Next week? So soon?"

"The sooner, the better," he replied, "and I am already writing to the Lord Chamberlain to say that you would like to present your stepdaughter at the second Drawing Room. I am sure that the first is already fully booked."

"Oh, my Lord, just how kind you are. How very very kind," Amalita exclaimed.

The Marquis put his hand over hers.

"I want to be kind to you," he said, "not only because you were the wife of my old friend but also because you are very beautiful. I find it so sad to see you in mourning. I would hope, Lady Maulpin, that you will wear colours that will enhance the perfection of your skin and your very lovely hair."

Amalita stared at him in surprise.

She realised that he was deliberately flattering her.

He wanted to console her for the loss of the man he himself had loved.

~83~

She was wearing black tonight because she thought it was too soon to appear in any way frivolous.

Also she felt that in black she looked older than she would have done in her mother's gowns.

She smiled at the Marquis and explained,

"I have always disliked black and so, to please you, I will wear bright colours. It is a mistake to live in the past when there is so much to look forward to in the future."

"Now that is a very sensible thing to say," the Marquis replied approvingly, "and that is just what we will do, my dear, you and I. I was praying, as I looked at your pretty stepdaughter tonight, that my son would realise that she is in every way different from that creature who was sitting on his other side."

She had not missed seeing that Lady Hermione had kept both the Earl and the gentleman sitting on her other side enthralled with her conversation and flirting.

She managed to amuse them all through dinner.

They were halfway through the menu before the Earl had turned and spoke to Carolyn.

Whatever she had replied had made him laugh.

This, Amalita thought, was definitely a hopeful sign.

But only a minute later Lady Hermione had recovered his attention.

After that he spoke to Carolyn only the once or twice before the dinner was finished.

Amalita had in fact not in any way wished to depress the Marquis. She hoped that he was not aware that so far his plotting and planning had been unsuccessful.

He talked about the ball he was giving and the people he was inviting.

At least a dozen of them were names she recognised as being in her father's address book.

"I am so excited about your party," she enthused. "I can only pray, my Lord, that Carolyn and I will not be a disappointment to you."

"You could neither of you ever be that," the Marquis asserted. "And I am so hoping to make my son see sense. Surely he is aware that Lady Hermione is of no use to him and she would be wholly detrimental to his character, his career and to the position that he will eventually hold as the Marquis of Garlestone."

He spoke so violently that Amalita said quickly,

"We can only pray and that is – something I promise – I will do for you."

CHAPTER FOUR

The Earl yawned as if he was feeling tired.

It was not surprising, considering he had just enjoyed three hours of fiery and passionate love-making with Lady Hermione.

He was thinking that it was time he dressed and went home.

As a rule the Earl disliked making love to a woman in her husband's house.

But, as Lord Buckworth was seldom in London, he had broken this rule.

Lady Hermione's house was just off Park Lane and it was therefore very convenient for him.

He yawned again and a soft cooing voice beside him purred,

"Darling wonderful David, I have to tell you that now Lionel is worse. The doctors say that it is only a question of days before he dies."

The Earl stiffened.

"If that is what you have been told," he then replied, "surely you should be with him?"

"What is the point?" Lady Hermione asked. "He does not recognise me now and the doctors and nurses are very efficient."

She moved a little nearer and her long fingers touched the Earl's bare skin before she said,

"You know what that means, darling? I shall be free!"

The way she spoke made the Earl instantly become aware of danger.

It was as if there were red lights dancing in front of his eyes and bells ringing in his ears.

After a definite pause, he said,

"It will soon be dawn. I must go home."

"Very soon when I will be free," she answered, "I can then keep you with me all the time and there need be no question of you leaving me."

With an effort the Earl climbed out of the bed.

Lady Hermione tried to stop him from doing so, but as her fingers slipped away, she said,

"Why are you in such a hurry? I want to talk to you."

"At this very late hour," the Earl said coldly, "there is really little to discuss."

"Not where we are concerned," she replied. "You do know, of course, David, without my putting it into words what I want and we will be very, very happy."

Next the Earl had slipped on his shirt.

He buttoned it down the front, looking into the mirror over the mantelpiece as he did so.

Then he said,

"If you are thinking that you and I might be married, Hermione, let me make it very clear to you, I would never marry anyone my father disapproved of."

Lady Hermione sat up in bed.

"That is a ridiculous thing to say?" she objected. "We all know that parents are jealous when their offspring fall in love."

The Earl was now dressing quickly and, as he put on his long, dark evening trousers, he said,

"I am devoted to my father and, as I have just said, I would never do anything to upset him."

"And you think I would upset him?"

"To be frank, Hermione," the Earl replied, "it would upset him enormously. That he does not approve of you is hardly surprising."

"Now you are being horrid to me!" Lady Hermione protested in what she thought was a very childlike voice. "I love you, David, and I swear that when I am your wife I will make you very happy, so happy that nothing else will be of any significance."

The Earl then shrugged himself into his smart tightly-fitting tail-coat.

And as he looked in the mirror to sweep back his dark hair, he said,

"We will talk about all this another time, but there is really nothing more to say. And I think, unless you wish to shock the Social world more than you have done already, you should be at your husband's side when he dies."

As he spoke, he walked across the room towards the bed.

Lady Hermione held up her arms.

"Kiss me goodnight, my adorable David," she begged. "You cannot leave me unhappy and forlorn."

She looked anything but forlorn, but the Earl made no comment.

He merely took one of her hands in his and raised it perfunctorily to his lips.

Then he said,

"Thank you, Hermione. Goodnight."

He had reached the door before she cried out,

"So when shall I see you again? I really must see you tomorrow. Please dine with me or shall I dine with you?"

Before she had spoken those last words, the Earl had closed the door.

She heard his footsteps going rapidly down the stairs.

For a moment or two she wondered if she should run after him.

Then she knew that he could evade her quite easily by opening the front door and walking into the street before she could stop him.

Petulantly she beat her pillows with her clenched fists.

She knew, although she would never acknowledge it, that the Earl had no intention of marrying her.

He had told her often enough that he had no wish to be married.

In the Clubs he was knows as the 'Elusive Bachelor'.

'How can he do this to me?' Lady Hermione asked herself furiously.

She punched her pillows again and again.

But she knew in her heart that she was just another woman who the Earl had amused himself with.

But he was everything that she wanted in a husband.

It was not only that he was so rich and would be the Marquis of Garlestone one day.

It was also because he excited her more than any other man had ever done.

She had believed that he would never be able to leave her.

Lady Hermione had sent many men away when she was tired of them and some had been sad and some angry, some vowing that one day she would suffer as they were suffering.

'That is what is happening to me now,' she thought.

She turned over to lie on her back, looking up at the ceiling.

She was now planning and plotting what she would do when that tiresome old man who was dying in the country had finally gone.

When she was totally free, she would somehow force the Earl to make her his wife.

She refused to accept that he would dispense with her as his mistress.

The ardency and great fervour of their love-making had convinced her that physically she was his.

However, she had always known that there was a part of him that could never be hers, something that she did not understand.

Every other man with whom she had come in contact had been so wholeheartedly at her feet.

Sometimes when she had wished to be rid of them, she had almost to cut them loose from her.

Even then, however brutal she had been, they would crawl back because she was so irresistible.

'If I lose David, I shall kill myself!' she said to herself dramatically.

Then she laughed.

How could she imagine for a moment that he would be able to resist her?

Nor was it possible that he would desire her no less than she desired him.

'I was rather too impatient,' she admonished herself. 'I should have waited until Lionel had died before telling him that I was ready to be his wife.'

It was something that she had never said to any other man.

She had imagined that the Earl would be as elated as she was at the thought of their belonging to each other.

Then there would be no necessity for him to go home before dawn.

'He will most certainly be back here tomorrow,' she thought with a confident smile.

Pulling the sheets up over her naked body, she closed her eyes and went to sleep.

*

Walking back through the empty streets to Park Lane, the Earl found that the coolness of the night air was very refreshing.

It struck him that he was tired of the exotic perfume that Hermione always used. It remained persistently on his body until he had his bath.

He also thought, rather unexpectedly, that he was tired of having to walk home just before the sun rose.

It would be a relief to climb into an empty bed in the quietness of his own room.

It was stupid, but it had never occurred to him until now that Hermione would want to marry him.

He wondered how he could have been so foolish.

He should have realised that once she was free there was no one who would make her a more desirable second husband than himself.

He could not remember in all his many affairs when a woman had actually asked to be his wife.

The majority of them had said,

"If only we had met earlier, before I was married."

They said it wistfully and plaintively and sometimes even angrily.

The Earl always had to prevent himself from replying that if they had met when she was a *debutante*, he would not have given her a second glance.

They had wept when he left them, but they had always known that the love affair must eventually come to an end.

Most of them had been careful of their reputations and they ensured that their husbands did not feel affronted and insulted by the Earl's attentions.

Hermione's husband was already a sick man when the Earl first met her.

He had, therefore, not thought that he was in any way encroaching on any possession that Lord Buckworth was incapable of appreciating.

"Married!"

He was in a situation, he thought, as dangerous as any he had faced in all of his life.

As he walked on, he told himself that being married to Lady Hermione would be undiluted hell.

She was everything that no man would ever want in his wife and that she should take over his mother's place as the Chatelaine of Garle was unthinkable.

She was beautiful, no one could deny that.

She was so physically alluring and the most insatiable woman he had ever known.

Yet now, he admitted to himself that if he was honest, he was slightly ashamed of being attracted to her.

He had been interested in her in the first place because of all he had heard about her from other men.

She was notorious for her behaviour and the manner in which she flouted all convention.

She apparently never gave a single thought as to what was being said about her.

No one could argue that she was not an outstanding personality or that her blood was not blue.

She had inherited a place in Society that could not be denied her.

At the same time the Earl admitted again that he had been extremely stupid.

Hermione had reached an age at which, if her husband died, she would wish to remarry without much delay.

Naturally it would have to be to a man who could give her a position in Society which was unassailable.

The Earl knew a number of hostesses whose doors were closed to Lady Hermione.

It was rumoured that the Queen had struck her off her list for the balls and other State functions at Buckingham Palace and Windsor Castle.

He had not discovered if this was true, but the Earl felt sure that it was.

Apart from anything else, just how could he possibly marry a woman who would turn out to be a disgrace to his father's name?

It would be unthinkable for her to take the place that the Marchionesses of Garlestone had traditionally held at Court.

'I have been a blind fool,' the Earl chided himself as he turned into Park Lane.

It was then, as he neared his father's house, that he found himself unexpectedly thinking of Lady Maulpin.

For the past two years the Earl had been protective of his father and, without a wife to restrain him, the Marquis had become almost absurdly generous.

He could not refuse anybody who approached him for help.

There were literally dozens of young men to whom the Marquis had behaved in a fatherly manner when they were in trouble.

He paid their debts and sent them abroad if they were involved in a scandal.

He even, on one special occasion, had prevented one impertinent youngster from fighting a duel.

At first the Earl had just been amused by his father's concern for other people, in particular the very young.

Then he realised that the Marquis was going too far.

He had consulted his father's Solicitors and they told him that his father was spending far too much money on wasters who had turned to him for financial help.

The Earl had accepted his father's open-handedness as he understood that he was lonely without his wife.

But, although the Marquis did not realise it, the Earl knew that he was being taken advantage of by those who he had been so generous to.

It was natural therefore, when his father received Lady Maulpin's letter, for him to be highly suspicious.

"So why on earth should they come to you, Papa?" he had asked his father. "After all you have not even seen Sir Frederick for a long time."

"Friendship does not depend upon time," the Marquis said. "He was always such a very good friend to me and, however many years passed without our seeing each other, we always seemed to pick up the conversation where we had left off."

"Of course I do understand," the Earl agreed. "But Sir Frederick is one thing and his widow and daughter quite another."

"But, of course, I must have them here," the Marquis insisted. "How can I refuse?"

As he had no wish to upset his father, the Earl had not pressed his objections.

He had thought that if he should find that these people were over-demanding or fast becoming an encumbrance, he would somehow have to get rid of them.

He had imagined that the new Lady Maulpin would be a middle-aged woman of about forty and as she apparently had so few friends, she was doubtless plain and a bore.

Sir Frederick's daughter would be like all *debutantes*, gauche and tongue-tied. She would also be in need of the polish that she would achieve when she married.

Because he was determined to protect his father from unwelcome guests, the Earl had deliberately been at home when Amalita and Carolyn arrived.

The butler had announced them.

When they come into the room, he had thought that there must be some mistake.

They could not possibly be the two women who were coming to London from the country.

Carolyn was undeniably beautiful.

He had not expected that Sir Frederick, even with his good looks, could produce such a daughter.

But Lady Maulpin was an enigma.

He had been aware that she was a little nervous when she arrived, which in many ways was understandable.

But he also knew a few minutes later that she regarded him in a somewhat hostile manner.

It was not because he was so conceited that he was surprised.

He could not imagine why she was not pleased to see him or find him as attractive as all women did.

As the Marquis knew, the Earl had a sharp and very astute brain.

The Prime Minister, Mr. Benjamin Disraeli, had said to him the previous week,

"Dammit all, David, you are exactly the man I want for the job. Why will you not go to Vienna as I have asked you to do?"

"Because, Prime Minister," the Earl answered him, "I know exactly what it will entail and at this moment I am enjoying myself in London."

"So I hear," Mr. Disraeli said dryly, "and, of course, I understand."

Then with his beguiling, or what his enemies called his 'cunning' manner, he went on,

"I have known you ever since you were a small boy, David, and you are so much cleverer and so much more intelligent than you will allow the world to know. That is why I need you. I do need your help at this moment."

"You will have to wait until the winter, or perhaps it may be a bit sooner," the Earl had replied. "But, of course, I find it a great compliment that you should wish me to do your 'dirty work' for you!"

Mr. Disraeli then threw himself back in his chair and laughed.

"You are really so incorrigible!" he complained. "One day I shall doubtless find something to tempt you with, but for the moment I can think of nothing except that the women of Vienna are all very beautiful."

"I have seen them," the Earl said, "and I promise you I will seriously consider the next proposition you put to me. For the moment, however, you will have to find another mug."

Mr. Disraeli laughed again.

Then he said,

"The trouble with you, David, is that you have been spoilt ever since you were in the cradle. Women find you irresistible. But I am not interested in your good looks and charm. It is your astute brain that I want."

"You are trying to catch me in a very clever way!" the Earl retorted. "Unfortunately for you I know your methods only too well. While Her Majesty has succumbed to your blandishments, I am still, albeit with some difficulty, able to resist them."

The Prime Minister then threw up his hands in a most impressive gesture.

"Very well," he said, "you win for the moment. But I shall not give up."

The Earl held out his hand.

"You have always been so very kind to me," he said, "and I know how much Papa admires you. When you have a minute to spare, come and see him. He is often lonely and so I have no wish to leave London at this moment."

Mr. Disraeli's eyes twinkled.

"Now you are using my own methods against me," he complained. "Very well, David, but do not forget I shall come knocking at your door and perhaps next time you will let me in."

As they walked towards the door, Mr. Disraeli put his hand on the Earl's shoulder.

"You are a naughty boy, David, but we all love you and well you know it."

The Earl had laughed as he went out into the corridor and Mr. Disraeli was smiling as he went back to his desk.

Now, as he neared his home as dawn broke, the Earl remembered how the Prime Minister had praised his brain.

He felt all the surer that there was something about Lady Maulpin that was not quite right.

He could not think what it was, but at the same time the suspicion intrigued him.

He was also intrigued by her beauty.

How could it be possible that anyone so lovely could be completely unknown and had never set foot in London?

He gathered from the conversation that she was about twenty-five or twenty-six.

Her late husband's very close friendship could never be forgotten.

How then could anybody who had seen her with him, or even just heard about her, have forgotten her?

As he walked into the house, the Earl tried to persuade himself that his ideas about her were unfounded.

Later in the morning he would find that neither of the women were as beautiful as they had seemed on arrival.

On an impulse he had then invited Lady Hermione and some of his friends to dinner.

His idea was to compare them with Lady Maulpin and her stepdaughter.

He had been certain that side by side with the lovely, sophisticated women with whom he spent all his time, they would pale into insignificance.

They would then look like the 'country cabbages' they actually were.

Although he well knew that his father heartily disliked Lady Hermione, he had asked her to dinner.

It was simply because he intended to see her later.

Another reason was that in doing so he had defied his conscience. It was pricking him because he had refused to help the Prime Minister.

Only by proving to himself that Lady Hermione was too irresistible to be left could he then justify his decision to stay in London.

She had certainly made a very theatrical entrance into the drawing room and he was well aware that there was a likeness between the two women.

They were both dark, they both had green eyes, and were about the same age.

When Lady Hermione had arrived with her feathered bustle fluttering behind her, he noticed that Lady Maulpin had given a little gasp and the Earl saw her gazing at the newcomer in astonishment.

Then he realised that, if it was just a question of points Lady Maulpin in her so elegant unflamboyant gown and wearing only some modest jewellery, was the winner.

When they had gone into the dining room, the Earl, to his surprise, found that Carolyn was sitting on his left.

He had a sudden idea why she had been seated there and he looked at his father and read his thoughts.

It made him want to laugh.

Could his father believe that he would be interested in a girl of eighteen who had never been to London before?

There was no doubt that Carolyn was beautiful.

Her golden hair and blue eyes were an Englishman's dream of what a really beautiful woman should look like.

But as it happened, the Earl had mainly been attracted to women with dark hair.

There had, however, been some fair heads and the odd redhead in his past.

Now, as he turned in at the gates of Garle House, he found himself smiling at his own thoughts.

His father had arranged the dinner table so that he had the devil on one side and an angel on the other.

'The good and the bad,' the Earl murmured beneath his breath and he wondered if anyone would think it funny except for himself.

Suddenly, as he walked up the steps to the front door, he could see Lady Maulpin's eyes watching him from the other end of the dinner table.

He was quite certain that she was thinking, as he had, that he was sitting between the good and the bad.

A sleepy footman let the Earl into the house.

In an hour's time the housemaids would be bustling downstairs to start cleaning the floors.

The Earl gave the footman his cape, his top hat and his cane.

"Goodnight, James," he said as he turned towards the staircase.

"Goodnight, my Lord," James replied.

The Earl walked along the corridor towards his room.

Most of the candles in the sconces had already been extinguished and there were, however, enough left alight for him to see his way clearly.

He passed the door of the room where Lady Maulpin was sleeping and he wondered what she would think if she knew that he had returned home so late.

He had the idea that despite her age, she was ignorant of the ways of the great Social world and of the men and women who were her contemporaries.

Then he told himself that he was being imaginative.

What he was telling himself was sheer nonsense.

Every woman he knew and especially any as beautiful as Lady Maulpin looked at every man as a prospective lover and she merely considered on which of them she would bestow her favours.

'That innocent look is very effective,' the Earl mused, 'but I am not such a 'greenhorn' as to be deceived by it.'

He had told his valet not to wait up for him and so he undressed himself and climbed into bed.

As he did so, he was thinking that, if he wished to forget Hermione, he could not do better than to turn his attention to the lovely Lady Maulpin.

She was here in the house and perhaps he had been remiss in not paying her the attention that she would have expected as a house guest.

Carolyn was clearly his father's idea for getting him away from Lady Hermione but he had nothing in common with a girl so young.

Furthermore she doubtless had little to say to anyone but platitudes.

If Lady Maulpin had been the wife of Sir Frederick, she must at least be intelligent.

The Earl had not seen him for years but he was known as a brilliant, clever and charming man whom everybody loved.

He would not have married, the Earl reasoned, unless the woman he chose as his wife had something in her that was different.

The more he thought of it, the more he decided that Lady Maulpin was worth exploring.

He still could not understand why she had looked at him in a slightly hostile manner when they first met.

Now he thought of it, she had seemed to avoid him when dinner was over.

There was nothing he could actually put his finger on.

And yet when he had made an effort to talk to her, she had been engaged with somebody else.

Even stranger she had not seemed in the least eager to join his party when they left Garle House.

Carolyn had certainly enjoyed herself.

He had left her in the care of his young cousin and he thought that they were just the right age for each other.

Anyway it would have been very difficult for him to do anything different with Lady Hermione clinging to him like a leech and she had made quite sure that he danced only with her.

*

The Earl should have fallen asleep.

Instead he asked himself why Lady Maulpin had been so obviously content to stay behind with his father.

He was aware that at dinner she was watching him and thinking disparagingly of Lady Hermione.

The indication was, of course, that like his father she thought that Carolyn would make him a suitable wife.

The Marquis had surely told her that he had married when his wife was not yet eighteen.

The Earl had loved his mother deeply and had been broken-hearted when she died.

He was studying at Oxford University at the time.

He could remember it only too well when he was told that she was dead and that he felt as if the sky darkened.

The domes and spires of Oxford had crashed to the ground.

The Earl had known exactly what his father must be feeling without her.

He had done everything he could to rouse him from the depression that at first he had sunk into.

It was after that that the Marquis had started to be so generous to those who turned to him for help.

While the Earl was grateful for anything that made his father happy, he was very determined that he should not be imposed on.

He well knew how the word had gone round London that, if it was just a question of money, the Marquis would give it liberally.

If it was an appeal for introductions, or a visit abroad, then the petitioner never asked in vain.

Now the Earl was aware that his father intended to give a party to introduce Carolyn and Lady Maulpin to the fashionable world.

He was also arranging for the girl's presentation at Court and would undoubtedly provide her with anything she required, even the right sort of gown that would be necessary.

'As long as it is not a Wedding gown!' he thought to himself.

He closed his eyes and began to fall asleep.

Suddenly he found himself wondering yet again how it was possible for Lady Maulpin to look so innocent.

It was as if she was an unmarried girl who just knew nothing about love.

CHAPTER FIVE

"I have had such a lovely day" Carolyn announced to the Marquis when she came down the stairs to dinner.

"I am delighted to hear it. What have you done?"

"We went out to luncheon with those nice people you introduced us to," Carolyn replied. "Then we watched the polo and your son played brilliantly."

"I thought you went shopping," the Marquis queried.

"Oh, we did that in the morning," Carolyn explained. "I have bought a glorious, glorious gown for your party and if you don't like it, I shall just sit in a corner and cry."

The Marquis laughed.

"I am sure that is something that will not happen and you will undoubtedly be the belle of my ball."

"I do hope so," Carolyn smiled, "but, as my s -- my stepmother said, there is a lot of competition in London."

She stumbled over the word 'stepmother', caught her sister's eye and looked embarrassed.

It was difficult when she was excited to remember that Amalita was not the same age as she was.

When they were alone, they were just girls together, enjoying excitements that they had never known before.

Amalita had most certainly bought the most beautiful gowns for Carolyn that she could have ever imagined.

Very obedient to the Marquis's wishes, she took back the black gown and changed it for two others in different colours.

The shop was very obliging and she soon realised that it was not the Marquis who had the reputation for buying expensive presents for women but the Earl.

It was not so much what the shop assistants said but what they implied.

She wondered what her mother would have said about ladies accepting expensive gifts from a man they were not married to.

To her surprise she learnt that the Earl was dining at home tonight when Carolyn and she were expecting to be alone with the Marquis.

'Perhaps,' Carolyn surmised when she heard of it, 'he feels as we do that he must go to bed early so as to be at his best tomorrow.'

Amalita thought that the Earl considered himself to be always at his best whatever he was doing.

At the same time like Carolyn she had been impressed at how brilliant he was on the polo ground.

It had been difficult to watch any other player and he looked so handsome and rode so well.

Whatever she might feel, she well knew that her father would have approved of him.

The door opened and the Earl walked in, looking, as he always did, magnificent in his evening clothes.

"Ah, here you are now, David," his father exclaimed. "I have been wondering why we are to be honoured with your presence this evening."

"That is easy to answer," the Earl replied. "I have not had a better invitation."

"That I don't believe." The Marquis smiled. "I saw a pile of letters for you this morning and thought that they must have had to put on extra postmen to deliver them all to the house."

The Earl sat down beside Carolyn.

"Did you enjoy the polo?" he asked her.

"I was just telling his Lordship that you played really brilliantly," she replied. "In fact it was little wonder that your team beat the others by five goals."

"It was very satisfying," the Earl said, "and now I am expecting you to win by five goals tomorrow evening at my father's ball!"

Carolyn laughed.

"It will be too terrible after what everybody has said if I am a flop."

"There is no chance of that," the Marquis interposed.

He was looking benignly at his son as he and Carolyn were talking together.

Amalita realised how very happy it would make him if what he hoped for came true.

The dinner was simply delicious and the Earl himself was unexpectedly entertaining throughout the meal.

He told them stories of his many adventures abroad.

Although he did not say so, Amalita guessed that he went on clandestine missions that somehow concerned the Prime Minister.

In fact she was sure that she was right when, after one story of his adventures in Turkey, the Marquis remarked,

"I heard that Benjamin Disraeli sent for you only the other morning. What did he want?"

"Need you ask?" the Earl replied.

"And you have agreed to do what he requested?"

The Earl shook his head.

"No, I refused. I so like being in London at this time of the year and, as you saw this afternoon, I enjoyed my game of polo enormously."

The Marquis frowned, but he did not say anything.

Watching the father and son, Amalita thought that the Marquis was very ambitious for the Earl.

As she already knew, he was so terrified that he would ruin his life by being too involved with Lady Hermione.

She wondered what the beautiful audacious lady was doing this evening since the Earl was not with her.

However, seeing how rapturously Carolyn listened to his stories, she thought that perhaps, when she had least expected it, the tide had turned.

After dinner was over they sat for a little while talking in the drawing room.

Then the Marquis suggested,

"I think we would all be wise to go early to bed. I am looking forward to tomorrow's Festivities as much as you are and I for one most certainly need my beauty sleep."

"You are very wise," Amalita said. "Come along then, Carolyn. We shall be late tomorrow and, like his Lordship, we will not be able to go to bed until the very last of the guests have left, of course reluctantly."

"I want you both to shine like stars!" the Marquis said.

"We will certainly do our best to please you," Amalita promised.

Carolyn made the Marquis a graceful curtsey and he said,

"I am glad you have had a happy day. I want this to be a very memorable visit for you and your stepmother."

"That is what it has been so far," Carolyn answered. "I am keeping a diary but I have now run out of adjectives to describe how wonderful everything is."

She turned to the Earl and said,

"I am sure that you are going to dream of how you managed to make that last goal and I shall certainly write about that."

"I am so honoured that I am to be included," the Earl replied.

Watching them Amalita felt that there was still that cynical slightly mocking look in his eyes.

Because it annoyed her, she walked towards the door without saying 'goodnight'.

Then she went to the hall without waiting for Carolyn to join her.

When they were alone upstairs, Carolyn put her arms around her sister's shoulders and said,

"It is so marvellous being in London and it is all due to you, Amalita. How could you be so clever as to have brought us here?"

She spoke in a whisper, but Amalita said quickly,

"Be careful!"

She was thinking as she spoke that despite his good humour, the Earl had, during the evening, looked at her penetratingly.

It was as if he suspected something about her.

She could not remember doing or saying anything that he might think strange.

At the same time she was sure that her intuition was right.

If he was not suspicious, then he was at least curious and that too could be dangerous.

The maid was waiting in her room to help her undress.

When she had left, Amalita pulled back the curtains and looked up at the stars.

"Thank you, *thank you*," she said beneath her breath.

She felt absolutely sure that her father had heard her.

How else could everything have gone so smoothly and the Marquis be so kind to her and Carolyn?

"Thank you, Papa," she said again.

She then closed the curtains and got into bed.

There was a small candelabrum of four candles on the table beside her bed.

Beside it was the Bible that her mother had given her.

She had promised when she was really quite small to read one verse or at least one line every night before she went to bed.

Because she felt that the Holy Book spoke to her, she would open it at random.

Then, with closed eyes, she would put her finger on the page.

Doing so now, she read,

"Ask, and it shall be given you, seek, and ye shall find.

Knock and it shall be opened unto you."

The words somehow seemed appropriate and Amalita hoped that it would be true.

Then, as she put the Bible down and was just about to blow out the candles, the door opened.

She looked up in some surprise, thinking that it must be Carolyn, who wanted her for some reason

To her astonishment, however, it was the Earl.

He closed the door behind him and advanced towards the bed.

"What – is the – matter? What has – happened?" she asked nervously.

As he drew nearer, she could see that he was wearing the kind of long frogged dressing gown that her father had always worn and it had made him look very Military.

As the Earl came nearer still, she asked him again,

"What is – it? Why are – you here?"

"You forgot to say 'goodnight' to me," he replied. "So I have to find out if you were just ignoring me or giving me an invitation."

Amalita stared at him in sheer astonishment.

"I-I don't – know what – you are saying," she said. "Please – go away. You have – no right – to come into my room."

The Earl sat down beside her on the bed.

He was in the light and she was partly shadowed by the curtain that fell from a canopy over her head.

He was able to see how really lovely she looked with her dark hair falling almost to her waist.

Her neck and arms were dazzlingly white against the darkness of it.

The Earl looked at her in admiration for a moment or two without speaking.

Then at last he said,

"You are so very lovely, so lovely that I cannot allow you to try and avoid me as you have been doing."

"I have not been avoiding you," Amalita contradicted him and then she added, "that may – not be – quite true, but you – should not – be here and if – you do want to – talk to me – we can talk tomorrow."

The Earl smiled.

"It is far easier when we are alone and unlikely to be disturbed and I think I can perhaps make you happy."

"I really don't – know what you are – talking about," Amalita said. "Please – please – go away. You know you should – not be in – my room."

"Who is to know and who is to say it is wrong?" the Earl replied.

"I – am saying – that," Amalita persisted, "and I never thought – I never – imagined that you would – come into my – bedroom like this."

"I was just thinking about you," the Earl said, "and I thought that now that you are a widow, perhaps you feel lonely at night. I also thought, maybe mistakenly, that you have a great deal to learn about love."

For a moment Amalita could think of nothing to say.

Her eyes seemed to fill her face.

Then, as the Earl bent forward, she thought that he was going to touch her.

She gave a little scream.

"Go away! Go – away at – once!" she cried. "How can you come here and talk to me like that. It is wrong – you know it – is very wrong!"

The Earl moved a little closer.

"It is nothing of the sort," he said. "And I only think, Amalita, that it would be very exciting to kiss you and I am quite sure that it would make you less lonely than you are at the moment."

"I am not lonely – I am *not*!" Amalita retorted. "And of course – you are not to – kiss me! Go away, go away at once."

The Earl then put out his arms, and now she struggled against him, turning her face from him.

She was not quite certain what he intended.

But she felt helpless and had no idea what she could do about it.

Then, as his lips touched her cheek, she asserted,

"You are – frightening me – there is – no one to help me – please – *please* leave me alone."

For a moment the Earl was still.

Then, to her surprise, he took her chin in his fingers and turned her face up to his.

"Are you really frightened?" he asked her.

He looked down at her, his eyes searching her face.

He was aware then that her lips were trembling and she was in fact desperately afraid.

"So you really are frightened," he said as if to confirm it to himself.

"I am very very frightened," Amalita said in a small voice. "Y-you are – so big and so powerful – and I just don't know how to – fight you. I only – know that my dear Papa would be extremely shocked at your being – here in my bedroom."

The Earl released her and sat up.

Then, with his eyes still on her face, he rose from the bed.

"I have never forced myself on any woman who did not want me," he said, "and my only excuse is that I did not realise that you were different."

He walked to the door as he spoke, letting himself out without looking back.

It had all happened so quickly.

Amalita could hardly recognise that he had come and said such strange things to her and then left.

"How – could he have – dared to – come to my room in that way?" she asked aloud.

At the same time she felt weak and, for some reason that she could not understand, felt like crying.

She lay trembling in the bed for some seconds before she told herself that it was her own fault.

She should have locked her door.

But just how could she have imagined for one moment that in a private house any man would come into a lady's room without being invited.

Then, as the thought came to her, she recalled what the Earl had said when he first came in.

Could he really have thought only because she had not bade him 'goodnight' that she was inviting him to come to her room?

Was that the way that Lady Hermione and the other women she had met in London behaved?

At the luncheon party she had attended today, some of the women, who were all known as 'beauties', had flirted openly with the gentlemen beside them.

She was quite certain that her mother would have been exceedingly shocked at their behaviour as well as the Earl coming into her bedroom in his father's house.

He had wanted to kiss her and teach her about love – whatever that might mean.

She was suddenly still.

Had he really thought and had he really believed that he could behave with her in the same way that he behaved with Lady Hermione?

Although Amalita was indeed very innocent, she just knew that Lady Hermione was very intimate with the Earl.

She thought, although it shocked her, that it must be in the same way that Yvette was intimate with her father.

'How dare he even think that I would behave in that shameless manner!' she stormed to herself,

Then, suddenly, she remembered that the Earl thought she was a widow and not a young and untouched girl like Carolyn

As she reasoned it out in her mind, she knew that not for one moment would he have contemplated going into Carolyn's bedroom.

But she was different because she was pretending to be five years older than she actually was and wearing her mother's Wedding ring.

It took her a little time to puzzle it out, but now she could see the picture only too clearly.

Her father had taught her to analyse her feelings and those of other people.

She could well understand that the whole episode was basically her fault for having deceived the Earl in the first place.

It still seemed to her extraordinary.

He imagined that he could walk into the bedroom of any woman he fancied, confident that she would welcome him with open arms.

But the fact definitely remained that as a supposedly experienced married woman she was to be treated in a very different way from any other unmarried girl.

'It – was really all my fault,' Amalita told herself.

She remembered her mother saying once when she was a small girl,

"It is always a mistake to lie. Telling lies makes you feel guilty and things can happen that are not foreseen, but are directly the result of the untruth."

This was something that she had not foreseen.

She had acted an untruth so as to deceive the Marquis.

She felt almost as if, because of the way that he had behaved, she and Carolyn should leave the house.

If they did so, she would then have to explain to the Marquis the reason why they were going.

After all his kindness, he would be upset and hurt.

'I – cannot do – that,' she thought. 'I shall – have to – stay.'

Then she wondered how she could meet the Earl and how embarrassing it would be after what had occurred.

She jumped out of bed and went to the window.

Once again she was looking up at the stars.

"What – shall I do – Papa?" she asked. "Please tell me – what I should do. It is all – such a big muddle."

She felt like crying because she had been feeling so happy when she had come to bed.

Then the Earl had spoilt it all.

Now she felt that her father was guiding her.

She knew at once that the only thing she could do was to behave as if it had not happened.

The house was a very large one and she could manage to avoid him and never in any circumstances be alone with him again.

Then she wondered if he was piqued at her behaviour and would insist on her and Carolyn leaving.

That might be even more disastrous if the Marquis started asking questions.

Once again she felt as if her father was speaking to her and he was telling her that whatever else he might be, the Earl was a gentleman.

He would certainly not speak to anyone of what had happened.

She was sure that he would not embarrass her more than she was already.

Finally, feeling a little comforted, Amalita pulled the curtains and went back to bed.

She blew out the candles, but it was a long time before she finally fell asleep.

*

In his own room the Earl was asking himself how he could have been such a fool and also so conceited.

It had never struck him for a moment that any woman, especially somebody as beautiful as Amalita would reject his advances.

He was used to women falling into his arms almost before he knew their names.

Women like Hermione pursued him relentlessly.

He could not remember when he had been refused a kiss or repulsed when he had wanted to make love.

There was no doubt that Amalita really had been most astonished to see him in her room.

He was certain that her fear was genuine and he had at first thought that she was playing hard to get and starting a new game of intrigue.

He had not taken her protests seriously until he was aware that she was trembling.

Now he asked himself again how he could have been so stupid, how could he have forgotten that in the country this sort of situation did not occur?

And yet, she had been a married woman.

As he thought of it, he was suddenly still.

At the moment he had touched her, he had felt that she was very young, innocent and completely unsophisticated.

This seemed strange when he remembered hearing as a boy of Sir Frederick's charm.

He had heard talk from the servants and even from his father of his love affairs.

He had admired Sir Frederick tremendously and much enjoyed talking to him when he came to the house.

He could recall when he was about six or seven years old peeping through the banisters at the guests arriving for dinner.

After that his Nanny had left him to go for her own supper.

He had crept out of bed to watch from the Minstrel's Gallery the party eating in the dining room at Garle Park.

He had seen two very beautiful women glittering with jewels and fawning on Sir Frederick.

The Earl had told himself that they admired him, just as he did.

Sir Frederick was frequently a guest at Garle Park.

Once when the Earl was a year or two older he had seen him in the garden late at night, kissing a very lovely woman.

The moon had been shining on them and they were standing beside the fountain and young though he was, the Earl had felt that it was very romantic.

He thought of Sir Frederick as a White Knight.

He must have won his Princess after killing the dragon that had frightened her.

It all came back to him and he also recalled how Sir Frederick had disappeared to the country after he had been married.

They had seldom seen him again and told him then it was because he was so happy that he had no wish to come to London.

"When a man is in the Garden of Eden," the Marquis had said poetically, "he has no wish to go back again to the wilderness!"

Thinking it over in detail, the Earl remembered that Sir Frederick's first wife, and he knew that Carolyn was like her, had died.

He must have then married Amalita.

Was it possible, because he was much older than she was, that he had left her untouched?

It seemed too incredible.

Suddenly, like a light shining in the darkness, the Earl could hear Amalita saying,

" – Papa would be very shocked at your being here."

She had been speaking about her father, of course, but surely it would have been more natural for her to say,

"'Frederick would be very shocked'!"

He found himself puzzling over what seemed to be a strange conundrum until he eventually fell asleep.

*

When Amalita woke in the morning, she then recalled what had happened the night before.

It seemed so incredible that she thought it must have been a dream and a not a very pleasant one.

She felt her heart beating frantically again and a blush coming to her face.

How could she meet the Earl again?

'What shall I say to him? And what – shall I do?' she asked.

The maid who had pulled back the curtains came to the bedside.

"His Lordship thought, my Lady," she said, "that you and Miss Maulpin should 'ave your breakfast in bed this mornin'. 'E suggests you rest 'cause you be so late last night."

"How kind of his Lordship," Amalita murmured.

She was glad, not to rest in bed but because she would not have to go down to breakfast and encounter the Earl.

She heard a footman put her breakfast tray on a table outside the door and the maid went to collect it.

Putting it down on a table that she had arranged by the bed, the maid said,

"I 'opes you've got everythin' you wants, my Lady, but if not, just ring the bell and I'll fetch you whatever you requires."

"I am sure I shall not want anything more," Amalita replied. "And I shall grow fat if I stay here much longer."

The maid laughed.

"I do 'opes not, my Lady. We was just sayin' in the servants' 'all as you've got the smallest waist of any lady as has stayed 'ere."

As she finished speaking, there came a knock on the door.

The maid opened it and there was then a muffled conversation with somebody outside.

She came back carrying a small parcel in her hand.

"I've bin told as to give you this, my Lady," the maid said.

Amalita took it from her, wondering what it could be.

It was too early to have come by post.

It was wrapped in white paper and tied with a bow of ribbon.

She thought that perhaps the Marquis had sent her a present.

She opened the parcel carefully.

When she had done so, she found that inside there was a single orchid.

It was pure white and quite perfect..

As she looked at it in surprise, she saw that there was a card attached to it.

It read,

"Forgive me."

As she read it, she felt her heartbeats quicken.

The colour came and went in her cheeks.

He had apologised.

This was something that she had not expected for she was sure that he had never done so before.

Quite suddenly her feelings towards the Earl seemed to change.

He was no longer a large menacing figure frightening her until she felt that she could not escape from him.

Instead he was a man who was big enough to admit that he had made a mistake and then to say he was sorry.

'Papa was right,' she told herself. 'He is a gentleman and as a gentleman he has done the right thing.'

She put the orchid down beside her.

Now she began to feel excited about the day that lay ahead.

She thought about the party to come in the evening and the very beautiful gowns that she and Carolyn were to wear.

It was all thrilling.

The black cloud that had for the moment eclipsed the sunshine had gone.

She felt happy. Very very happy.

And all because the Earl had done the right thing.

The white orchid which was lying beside her was very beautiful.

CHAPTER SIX

Amalita looked round the ballroom and thought that nothing could be more attractive and enchanting.

The women in their beautiful gowns looked exactly like swans.

Their tiaras glittered as they were swung around the room in the arms of their partners to a dreamy waltz.

Amalita had put on her mother's tiara, thinking that it would make her look older.

She well knew that the Marquis admired her and he had insisted that both she and Carolyn should be standing beside him as he received his guests.

Amalita was a little afraid that somebody would arrive who would remember that her father had two daughters.

Then she reassured herself that it had all happened a long time ago.

Also her father and mother had always preferred to be by themselves in the country.

It pleased her when the older of the Marquis's friends said such charming things to her and Carolyn about their father.

They said that they had always believed him to be the most attractive man in London.

The Marquis kept them with him until he thought that everybody of importance had arrived.

Then Carolyn was swept off to the ballroom to dance with one young gentleman after another.

Amalita found that she was never without a partner and the orchestra was excellent, playing all the melodious times that had recently become fashionable.

Watching the guests with interest in the flower-filled room, Amalita thought nothing could be more romantic.

Some of the windows opened out into the garden and the Marquis had arranged for Chinese lanterns to be hung from the boughs of the trees and the paths were outlined with small fairy lights.

Amalita was certain that Carolyn really was the belle of the ball.

Her gown was pure white, caught up at the side of the bustle with bunches of pink roses and a sash matching the colour of her eyes encircled her small waist.

In fact she was spectacular.

Flushed with excitement she looked like a child at its first pantomime.

Amalita was not surprised when one man after another said to her,

"Your stepdaughter is surely the most attractive girl I have ever seen!"

The Earl had presided at the end of the table at dinner and on each side of him there were two of their most distinguished lady guests, a Marchioness and a Countess.

There was no question tonight of it being a choice between 'the Good and the Bad'.

He was looking even more distinguished than usual because he was wearing several decorations.

A cross hung round his neck on a red ribbon.

Amalita longed to know what it represented, but she thought, however, that to ask would make her seem very ignorant.

Soon after the music had started, the Earl asked her to dance.

For a moment she hesitated, thinking that he should ask Carolyn first.

Afraid of seeming interfering, she accepted at once his invitation and he took her onto the dance floor.

He danced very well.

She only hoped that he would not realise that she was not at all an experienced dancer.

She had, of course, danced at all the children's parties they had attended, but they were very few and far between in Worcestershire.

She had, however, often danced with her father while her mother played the piano.

"You must be like thistledown in my arms," he had said, "and that is exactly how your mother felt when I first danced with her. After dancing with her at endless balls every other woman seemed like a sack of potatoes!"

Amalita wondered now, as he danced with her, what the Earl was thinking.

When the dance came to an end, he said,

"I thought your feet never touched the ground and you were flying rather than dancing."

They were the first words he had spoken to her since they had gone onto the dance floor.

As she smiled up at him, he asked in a low voice,

"Am I forgiven?"

"Of – course," Amalita agreed quickly.

She could not help the colour that then came into her cheeks and her eyes flickered.

Then she said,

"Thank you – for the beautiful orchid."

"I thought it was like you," the Earl explained.

There was no chance of his saying anything more.

A Peer, who Amalita knew was of great importance in the Political world, came up to the Earl to say,

"I hope that you are not going to monopolise the most beautiful woman in the room. Please introduce me."

With that he swept Amalita onto the dance floor and the Earl walked away.

As she finished dancing with the Peer, who paid her extravagant compliments, she looked round for Carolyn, but there was no sign of her.

Amalita thought that maybe she might have gone into the garden and she wondered if she should have warned her not to stay there too long with any one gentleman.

This, as she knew, could earn her a bad reputation.

Amalita would have been surprised if she had known where Carolyn was at that moment.

She had run away from the ballroom into one of the sitting rooms. It was one arranged for those who wished to talk rather than dance.

She was standing by the fireplace, looking down at the flowers that filled it.

The door opened and Timothy Lambton came in.

"I thought I saw you at the other end of the corridor," he said. "Why are you here? You should be dancing."

"I don't – want to dance this – dance," Carolyn said in a low voice.

Timothy went to stand beside her.

"Why not?" he asked.

She did not reply and after a moment he said,

"Do tell me why, Carolyn. Why do you not want to dance this particular dance?"

"Because," she replied hesitatingly, "it is – with the – Earl."

"And you don't want to dance with him?"

She shook her head.

"Why ever not?" Timothy asked. "What has he said to you?"

He spoke sharply and, when Carolyn remained silent, he went on,

"If he has upset you, I will knock him down. I know Cousin David's behaviour with women only too well and it is something I will not let happen with you."

Carolyn gave a little cry.

"It – is not that, it is not anything that he said, but – your uncle – "

Timothy took hold of her arm and then drew her to the sofa.

As they both sat down, he said in a quiet kind voice,

"Now, what is all this about? Tell me what has upset you."

"I-I don't – think I ought to – tell you."

"I thought you could trust me, Carolyn."

"I do – *I do*," she said, "but what – he said was – a shock."

Timothy then took her hand in both of his and held it tightly.

"I cannot believe that my uncle would wish to upset you, Carolyn," he said. "So tell me exactly what he said and then we can sort it out between us."

Because he spoke so beguilingly, Carolyn muttered,

"I went – up to him – after I had – been dancing and said, 'thank you – thank you for this wonderful party. It is so exciting and I am enjoying myself enormously'."

Her voice died away and Timothy asked,

"And what did my uncle reply?"

"He – said," Carolyn replied in a voice that he could hardly hear,

"'I hope that the next party I shall give here will be for your marriage. I just know that you and David will be very happy together'."

Carolyn's voice broke on the last words, and she said,

"Now I – understand what he has been thinking and why I kept – being put – beside the Earl at mealtimes – but I do *not* want – to marry him – he frightens – me."

Her voice was piteous and Timothy was silent.

Unexpectedly he rose and pulled her to her feet before he said,

"I want to show you something."

She did not ask questions, but allowed him to lead her from the sitting room and down the corridor.

They did not go in the direction of the ballroom, but the opposite way.

Timothy led her to a side staircase and still without speaking he took her up it.

They climbed from the first floor to the second and from the second to the top floor, where the attics were.

Content to do what Timothy wanted, Carolyn let him lead her along an attic until they came to some steps.

He opened the door at the top of them.

Feeling somewhat bewildered, Carolyn wondered why he was taking her out onto the roof.

It was a flat roof and there was a balustrade on the side of it.

Timothy led her to it.

Carolyn saw there lay in front of her a most incredible panorama.

The sky overhead was filled with stars and there was a full moon throwing its light over London.

Below were the trees of St. James's Park and beyond were the Houses of Parliament beside the Thames.

Then she could see the river, silver in the moonlight and winding its way towards the sea.

The lights on the bridges crossing it were reflected on its smooth surface.

It was all so lovely that Carolyn could only stare at it until Timothy asked softly,

"What does this mean to you?"

"It is – beautiful! The most – beautiful view I have – ever seen!" Carolyn answered. "It makes me – feel as if it is part of my – heart and – of my – soul."

She was speaking almost to herself or how she would have spoken to Amalita.

"That is what I wanted you to feel," Timothy replied, "and I have something to tell you, Carolyn."

"What is – it?" she asked with her eyes still on the river.

"I have been painting pictures," he replied, "and my Teacher, who is a well-known artist, is pleased with my work. What I intend to do is to travel all over the world, painting beauty like the scene you are looking at now."

"All over the world?" Carolyn questioned.

"I want to paint every scene that moves me as this is moving you," Timothy said. "Then I shall put it all into a book for people to see who cannot travel as I intend to do."

There was silence.

Then Carolyn said,

"I am sure – it is a – wonderful idea for you, but you are going away, are you – going alone?"

"Not if you will come with me," Timothy said quietly.

Carolyn turned towards him, her eyes were very wide in the moonlight.

"W-with – you?" she whispered.

"I did not mean to tell you so soon," Timothy replied, "but I fell in love with you the very moment I saw you. I thought, as you were so young and had seen so little of the world, that I ought to give you the chance to meet other men."

His fingers tightened on hers until they hurt.

Then he sighed,

"But I cannot risk losing you."

For a moment they just gazed at each other.

Then Carolyn asked in a very quiet voice,

"What do you want me to do?"

Timothy smiled.

"I am asking you to marry me, my darling. I may not be as grand as Cousin David, but I think we feel the same and think the same about beauty and I know that the world would be very beautiful with you."

Carolyn gave a cry of sheer happiness.

As she moved towards him, his arms went round her.

He held her very close, looking down into her eyes.

Now it seemed as if they held the stars in their hands.

"I worship you," he said a little hoarsely.

He held her even tighter and then he kissed her.

He was very gentle, knowing that it was the first time that she had ever been kissed.

To Carolyn it was as if the Heavens opened.

He took her into a world of beauty and love, of which she had always dreamt that one day she would find.

As he raised his head, she stammered,

"I – love you – but I did not know – I did until now."

Then Timothy was kissing her once again and there was only the moon, the stars and him.

*

At two o'clock the guests started to leave.

It was then that Amalita realised that she had not seen Carolyn for a long time.

It was, however, difficult in such a big crowd to keep track of anyone.

She had been very grateful as the evening progressed to realise that Lady Hermione had not been invited.

It was the Marquis's party and the Earl, who had not seen Lady Hermione for two days, had no idea that she was expecting him to take her to it.

Early on in the evening when he had finished dancing with Amalita a servant approached him.

'There be a lady at the door, my Lord," he said, "and she wants to speak to you urgently."

For a moment the Earl wondered who it could be.

However thinking it a mistake to ask questions of the servant, he went from the ballroom into the hall.

The front door was open and he could see a carriage outside.

It still did not strike him as to who it was until he went down the steps.

Then he recognised the Livery of the footman at the carriage door.

He opened it and the Earl looked inside.

Lady Hermione was elaborately gowned and wearing a diamond tiara in her dark hair.

"I have come to your party, darling David," she said, "but I am waiting for you to escort me inside."

"I am afraid that is impossible," the Earl replied.

"But why? What do you mean?" she demanded.

"In the first place I am not giving the party," the Earl explained to her carefully, "and, as you know, my father is giving it to introduce Carolyn to her father's friends."

"And the Marquis, of course, does not want me here," Lady Hermione said bitterly. "But it is your house too and I do *not* like to think that I am barred from anything, my dearest, that belongs to you."

Because the Earl thought that the footman could hear what they were saying, he climbed into the carriage.

He then sat down beside Lady Hermione and closed the door.

"Now, listen, Hermione," he began.

She flung herself against him, her hand going up to touch his cheek caressingly.

"Oh, darling, *darling*," she murmured, "I have missed you! How can you stay away from me? I waited for you all last night."

"We are concerned at the moment with tonight," the Earl replied, "and, as you are well aware, my father does not approve of you. I am sorry, Hermione, but you would not be a welcome guest at the party he is giving for a very young girl."

"I suppose you realise," she said spitefully, "that he is expecting you to marry that unfledged chick who has just come out of the egg! Can you just really imagine anything more boring?"

"As I have told you before," the Earl said quietly, "I intend to marry no one until I am obliged to have an heir and I assure you, I will never, in any circumstances, marry someone of whom my father disapproves."

Lady Hermione took her hand away from his face.

"How can you be so cruel," she asked, "so unkind? You know we would be very happy together."

"Not if it hurt my father," the Earl stipulated firmly.

He reached out towards the door handle.

"I just cannot leave the party, Hermione. We will talk about this another time."

As he finished speaking, he pushed the door open and jumped out of the carriage.

She waited for him to turn back and say 'goodnight'.

Instead he walked up the steps and went in through the front door.

For one moment she considered running after him and forcing herself upon the party.

Then she remembered if there was one thing that the Earl disliked, it was a scene.

It would be a great mistake to have one in front of the Marquis and the Earl's friends who did not approve of her.

The footman dutifully waited at the carriage door for his instructions.

In a voice that sounded harsh even to herself, she told him where to take her. It was to a house where she knew that there was a riotous and drunken party in full swing

The women present would not be of the same social standing as herself, but what did it matter?

The Earl was absolutely furious as he walked back to the ballroom.

Only Hermione, he thought, would have had the sheer audacity to come to a party that she had not been invited to.

He wondered how he could make her realise once and for all that their affair was at an end.

It was nothing unusual for him to find that his interest in a woman had waned abruptly.

Now he knew that Hermione had been a mistake from the very beginning.

He not only had no wish to see her again, but would make every effort to avoid coming in contact with her.

It was then, as he entered the ballroom, that he saw Amalita coming in from the garden.

She was silhouetted for a minute against the darkness.

The light of the moon and the many Chinese lanterns glittered on the jewels in her hair.

It made her seem as if she had just stepped down from the sky.

She looked, in fact, so lovely that the Earl could not remember when he had ever seen a woman look quite so entrancing.

At the same time she had an aura of spirituality.

It made her seem not human but part of some other world.

He walked towards her.

As he reached her, he knew that she was different in every way from any woman he had ever known before.

*

The hands of the grandfather clock in the hall were pointing to three o'clock as the last guests said 'goodbye'.

They thanked the Marquis most effusively for such a delightful evening.

"I am glad they have enjoyed themselves," he said to Amalita.

"How could they have done anything else?" Amalita asked.

"It was the most successful party you have ever given. Papa!" the Earl said. "I do fully congratulate you on your organisation and the fact that you invited exactly the sort of people that Carolyn should meet."

"And many of them remembered Sir Frederick," the Marquis said. "How could anybody forget him?"

He looked at Amalita and she smiled.

At the same time she was glancing around the empty ballroom and wondering to herself whatever could have happened to Carolyn.

She thought it remiss of her sister not to be there and she should have said 'goodnight' to all the people who had talked to her about her father.

Amalita was about to remark on her sister's absence.

Then she saw Carolyn and Timothy coming down the lit path from the far end of the garden.

They were walking hand-in-hand and Amalita thought that it was slightly indiscreet.

To her surprise they continued to hold hands as they reached the Marquis.

"Ah, there you are," the Marquis exclaimed. "There were quite a number of people waiting to say 'goodnight' to you."

"I am sorry," Carolyn said, "but I was with Timothy."

The Marquis then looked at his nephew, but before he could say anything, Carolyn said,

"Thank you, thank you for a wonderful party that I shall always remember – because it – gave Timothy and me the most – important moment – of our lives."

She looked up at Timothy as she spoke.

Then, as it suddenly began to dawn on Amalita what had happened, Timothy said,

"I want you to congratulate me, Uncle. Carolyn has promised to marry me!"

"Marry you?" the Marquis repeated.

It was obvious that such an idea had never entered his head.

Then Carolyn bent forward and kissed his cheek.

"Please give us your – blessing," she begged. "We are so very – very – happy."

The Marquis accepted the situation with what Amalita thought was an inborn dignity.

"So you are to be married!" he said. "Well, that is certainly a surprise. But, of course, I wish you both every happiness."

"We shall be *very* happy," Timothy said, "and we are going to go round the world so that Carolyn can help me with my pictures and the book that I told you I wanted to write."

"You told me," the Marquis answered, "but I did not take you seriously. Now I am sure that Carolyn will see that you finish it."

"She will contribute to it," Timothy said firmly, "and because it is to be a book about beauty, it will, of course, be dedicated to her."

As he spoke, he looked at Carolyn.

There was such a look of love in his eyes that Amalita felt the tears come into hers.

She had been standing aside and now Carolyn flung her arms round her sister's neck.

"Say you are pleased," she begged, "I know you like Timothy and – he is the most – adorable person in the – whole world!"

"Of course I am pleased," Amalita smiled.

She kissed Carolyn before she turned a little shyly to the Earl.

As if he understood why she felt embarrassed, he said,

"I think that Timothy is very wise to marry anyone so lovely before she is spoilt by too many compliments and is swept away from him by somebody else."

His eyes were twinkling as he spoke and Timothy held out his hand.

"Thank you, David," he said, "I knew that you would understand."

"It only remains for you to tell me what you want for a wedding present," the Earl replied, "and, of course, Papa will give the Reception here, which means another party as good as the one we have just enjoyed."

Carolyn gave a little whoop of joy.

"Will you do – that?" she asked the Marquis. "We could not ask many people to our house in Worcestershire – and besides, I want you to give me away."

"I shall be very honoured to do so," the Marquis said as he smiled, "and now, children, I think we should all go to bed. The servants will want to lock up and I personally am exhausted."

"We are all tired," the Earl agreed, "and we can talk it over tomorrow morning, including Carolyn and Timothy's forthcoming Wedding."

"Well, come along, come along," the Marquis said.

As they went up the, stairs, Amalita wondered if the Marquis was disappointed.

But she could not help thinking that Carolyn would be so much happier with Timothy than she would ever have been with the Earl.

For one thing they were nearer to each other's ages.

Also she was certain that Timothy was a lovable and quiet person who would never earn the sort of reputation that the Earl had.

He would eventually become Lord Lambton.

In the meantime they could enjoy themselves without restrictions.

Later on they would have to fulfil the demands of the position that Timothy would inherit.

She felt sure as she reached her bedroom that both her father and mother would have approved of the marriage.

The Marquis might have had other ideas, but he had not been thinking of Carolyn's happiness.

He was intent only on getting his son away from the clutches of Lady Hermione.

'I have to think of Carolyn,' Amalita told herself, 'and I must take care that nothing spoils her happiness.'

She gave a little sigh.

'Although the Social world may not agree with me, I never felt for a moment that Carolyn would be a suitable wife for the Earl.'

The mere thought of her sister coming in contact with a woman like Lady Hermione made her shudder.

She indeed knew that Carolyn was far too young and inexperienced to deal in any way with a woman like her.

To Amalita she personified everything in the world that was wicked.

Timothy kissed Carolyn's hand lightly and then bade her 'goodnight'.

As he did so in a whisper that no one else could hear, he told her again that he loved her.

He was staying the night in his uncle's house because his father and mother lived outside London at Wimbledon and it was too late to go so far.

As he went off to his own bedroom, Carolyn kissed her sister and said,

"I will tell you all about it tomorrow, but if we are to obey the Marquis, we must all go to bed."

"I agree that is sensible," Amalita said. "Goodnight, my dearest, and God bless you."

"He *has* blessed me already." Carolyn smiled. "How could anything be more wonderful than being married to Timothy?"

She kissed her sister again and ran across the corridor to her own room.

Amalita opened the door to her room.

Only then did she realise that the Earl, who had been behind them, had reached the top of the stairs.

She gave him one quick glance before she attempted to escape into her own room.

But before she could do so, he had reached her.

"Are you disappointed?" he asked.

She did not pretend to misunderstand him.

"It was your father's idea, not mine," she answered.

"I know," he said, "but I suspect that, like all women, you were thinking how important socially Carolyn would be."

He spoke somewhat provocatively.

"On the contrary," Amalita answered, "I want Carolyn to be as happy as her father and mother were."

She paused for a moment before she added,

"They wanted only to be together and that, believe it or not, is what I want for Carolyn."

"And what you would want for yourself too?" the Earl questioned in a grave voice.

"Of course I do," Amalita replied, "and so do you and so does anyone who has any sense. There is no value you can put on love, except that we all pray that one day it will be ours."

She spoke in a low and fervent little voice.

Then she felt that she had said too much.

She slipped through the door and shut it in the Earl's face.

Standing just inside her bedroom, she heard him walk away and then wondered if she had been rather rude.

But she told herself that at least she had spoken the truth.

How could he imagine, unless he was a fool, that the emotions he felt for somebody like Lady Hermione were love?

'When he watches Carolyn and Timothy together, he will realise what he is missing,' she mused.

She undressed quickly and climbed into bed.

As she did so, she found herself thinking not of the ball or of Carolyn but of the Earl.

However foolish he might be in wasting his time with Lady Hermione, he was undoubtedly the most handsome man she had ever seen.

He had stood out in the ballroom and she had found herself looking at him and not listening to what her partner was saying.

She thought that he was as good a host as his father and he had made very sure that everyone was enjoying the party.

He had left no one unattended.

She had noticed during the evening how he had talked to the older guests that the Marquis had invited, some of whom were his relatives.

They were mostly too old and slow to dance, but had sat watching and, of course, chatting away to each other.

The Earl had made a point of going up to them and whatever it was he had said to them obviously made them happy.

'There is a kindly streak in him,' Amalita admitted to herself, 'which I am sure that many men do not have.'

Then she asked herself who, if Carolyn was no longer available, the Marquis would choose as a suitable wife for his son.

She was wondering what the answer would be as she fell asleep.

CHAPTER SEVEN

Amalita awoke late the next morning.

She was having her breakfast when Carolyn came into the room.

"You are awake, Amalita," she said, "and is it not a wonderful, wonderful – day!"

"I am sure you must think so," Amalita replied.

Carolyn sat down on the edge of the bed.

"Timothy is taking me to meet his mother and father," she said. "They arrived back home from France only late last night, which was why they were not at the party."

"I am really sure," Amalita replied, "that they will be very thrilled that their son is marrying someone quite so charming."

"I hope so – I hope that is what they – will think," Carolyn said. "And you will not mind, darling, if we stay on for dinner? Timothy has so much to show me of his pictures that it will be a considerable bore to have to come back too quickly."

Amalita knew that Lord and Lady Lambton lived in Wimbledon.

She had already heard from the Marquis that his sister suffered from asthma in the winter and doctors thought the country air outside the City was better for her.

"I look forward to meeting her," Amalita had said.

"She is attractive and so like my mother," the Marquis replied. "She married when she was very young and was never as close to her parents as David is to me."

He spoke with a note of pride in his voice, which was always there when he spoke of his son.

Amalita had thought it touching and she said now to Carolyn,

"I must explain to your future father and mother-in-law that, although you and Timothy made up your minds in great haste, you really do love each other."

Carolyn smiled.

"I think Timothy will say that. Oh, Amalita, I am so lucky to have found somebody so wonderful and Timothy and I want to be married very soon."

She paused before she went on,

"Is it not so fortunate that the Marquis has said he will give the Reception here? You know that we could never get all those people into our house."

The way she spoke made Amalita feel worried.

She was wondering when and just how she could ever explain it to Timothy's father and mother that she was in fact Carolyn's sister.

That would mean telling the Marquis and, of course, the Earl as well.

She felt herself quiver at the thought of how sarcastic he would be about it.

"You have not told Timothy the truth?" she asked her sister hastily.

"Not yet," Carolyn replied. "I felt that I should ask you first, but after that I do *not* want to have any secrets from him in the future."

"No, of course not," Amalita agreed. "Just give me time to think out what we should do."

She felt despairingly that once Carolyn was married, she herself would have to go back to the country.

She would be alone in the house which had once been full of love and laughter.

It would be impossible for her to remain in London, either as Lady Maulpin or as herself.

'What shall I do?' she asked herself frantically.

Then she thought that it was one of those problems that would have to be solved later rather than sooner.

What was important now was that Carolyn was to be married.

'Whatever happens in the future,' she told herself, 'I must do nothing that would spoil her happiness.'

Carolyn then went off in a hurry to be with Timothy, kissing Amalita affectionately before she did so.

"And how are you planning to travel to Wimbledon?" Amalita managed to ask just before she left.

"Timothy came here in his father's carriage," Carolyn answered, "which, of course, is now back at Wimbledon. So today he is borrowing a chaise from the Marquis and driving it himself."

It flashed through Amalita's mind that she ought to be chaperoned. Then she thought that, as Carolyn was now engaged, it was unnecessary and it would be very stupid to suggest it.

"Tell him to drive carefully," she said instead.

"He will," Carolyn replied gaily and was gone.

Amalita got up slowly, thinking it strange that she had nothing to do.

Shopping was finished, except that very soon Carolyn would want some more gowns for her trousseau.

The party was over and so the household would now have to find something new to talk about.

For the past two days the Marquis had been explaining to her which of the people invited to the party had been friends of Sir Frederick.

She went downstairs to find that he was in his study.

"I am glad that you have joined me, Lady Maulpin," he said, "because I do want to talk to you about the young people. I think we must find them somewhere pleasant to live when they come back from their honeymoon."

Amalita looked at him questioningly and he said with a smile,

"I expect you have been told that Timothy is eager to go around the world painting pictures of places he thinks are beautiful and which will eventually appear in a book."

"Yes, Carolyn did tell me," Amalita agreed.

"It is what they intend to do," the Marquis carried on, "and I think it a good idea. It is always wise to travel when one is young and before one is tied down with too many babies."

Amalita laughed.

"I find it hard to take all this in," she said. "Last night Carolyn was a *debutante* appearing in the Social world for the very first time. Now you are talking about her being the mother of a number of children."

"These young move far too fast for me," the Marquis complained. "So now, Lady Maulpin, we are left with the problem of David and that terrible woman!"

Amalita sat down in a comfortable chair.

"I am so relieved that she did not come to your party last night," she said.

"So was I," the Marquis nodded. "I thought that David might try and persuade me to invite her, but to my relief he never mentioned it."

"Perhaps he has tired of her," Amalita suggested.

She did not really believe it, but thought that it would cheer up the Marquis.

He was such a kindly man and she could not bear to think of him worrying so over his son and so being made unhappy as the Earl was so involved with Lady Hermione.

The Marquis went to stand in front of the mantelpiece.

"I suppose it was stupid of me to think that David might marry anyone as young as your stepdaughter," he said. "At the same time she is so beautiful that I thought that he would not fail to be captivated by her."

"I don't want to be unkind," Amalita said, "but I think Carolyn will be far happier with Timothy, with whom she is in love and who is such a kind and gentle person."

"You are right, of course, you are right," the Marquis said. "It was foolish of me to have had any other ideas."

He sighed and then changed the subject.

"Now let's talk about you. You must tell me what you intend to do once Carolyn is married."

Amalita felt that this was rather dangerous ground so she merely said,

"I think for the moment I must concentrate on Carolyn and not worry about myself. There will be plenty of time to make decisions after we have bought her trousseau and you have been kind enough to give the Reception for her."

"She is pleased at what I suggested," the Marquis said, "and, of course, as Timothy is my nephew, I want to make them both happy."

"Just as you have made so many other people happy," Amalita said softly.

They talked until luncheontime and then had the meal alone together.

Afterwards Amalita thought that, as the Marquis was busy, she might as well lie down.

She went up to her bedroom and almost immediately fell asleep.

She slept peacefully until it was teatime.

Then she went downstairs to join the Marquis.

"I have been very busy," he said, "making lists of the people to be invited to the Wedding and planning a series of dinner parties so that Carolyn will be able to meet my relations."

He chuckled before he added,

"I am afraid that there are a great number of them and they will all be intensely curious about the girl my nephew is to marry."

"I do hope that they will not scare Carolyn," Amalita pointed out.

They talked about the Wedding until it was time to go up and change for dinner.

As Amalita had her bath, she was thinking it strange that she had not seen the Earl all day.

He was very likely playing polo and the Marquis had not said that he was expected back for dinner.

She thought it a very good thing that she was there.

Otherwise the Marquis would be alone with nobody to talk to. He was so kind and always thinking of others, she told herself.

She put on one of her prettiest gowns and then went downstairs.

There was still no sign of the Earl and, when she had joined the Marquis, she said,

"I expected the Earl to be dining with us tonight."

"David sent me a message earlier today to say that he had a number of engagements and that I was not to wait for him."

As if he thought that Amalita was looking critical, he added,

"He always lets me know whether he will be in or out and anyway this afternoon he was playing polo again."

Amalita knew then that she had been right in thinking that was what he was doing.

She would, however, have liked to discuss with him the party that had taken place last night.

Then she told herself that he was doubtless spending his time with Lady Hermione.

In a strange way it made her feel sad.

It also gave her another strong feeling that she did not understand or recognise.

When dinner was finished, she and the Marquis went into a small sitting room on the ground floor.

It was cosier than the large drawing room and it was a very attractive room, and had long French windows which overlooked the garden.

It was very warm and the Marquis stood looking out at the fountain throwing its water high up into the sky.

The stars were just coming out and a full moon was emerging from behind a cloud.

"I think you possess the most romantic garden anyone in London could have," Amalita exclaimed.

"I often think that myself," the Marquis replied, "but, alas, my dear, I am too old to be romantic except in my dreams."

"I am sure that is not true," Amalita said. "Anyway, you have plenty of exciting times to look back on."

"Of course I have," the Marquis agreed.

They walked back into the sitting room.

Then, just as they were once again looking at the list of Garle relations who were to be invited to meet Carolyn, the door opened.

Amalita looked up, thinking that it must be the Earl.

To her astonishment Lady Hermione then came into the room.

She was wearing a fantastic black gown trimmed with white and on her head she wore a black hat adorned with white feathers.

Amalita and the Marquis stared at her as she walked towards them.

"I have just learned, my Lord," she began in a quiet voice, "that my poor husband is worse and I am, therefore, taking your advice and leaving at once to be with him in the country."

"I am sure that is very sensible," the Marquis said as he rose to his feet.

"I have thought before I left," Lady Hermione went on, "that I should bring you a present to thank you for the delightful dinner I had with you the other evening. I have been very remiss in not writing to thank you."

She smiled beguilingly before she went on,

"Instead I have brought you a bottle of Lionel's most prized vintage port. I believe that there is very little left of it and I know that, because he has always admired you so much, he would like you to have this bottle."

She held out the bottle as she spoke and the Marquis took it from her.

"That is most kind of you," he said politely.

"You must promise me to drink it all yourself," Lady Hermione said. "My husband has always claimed that it is too good for young men who have not the experience to appreciate a really magnificent wine."

The Marquis looked at the bottle and then he said,

'Thank you very much. I know I shall enjoy it."

"David has told me how much you enjoy port," Lady Hermione said, "and thank you very much again for the other evening."

She held out her hand.

Then, after the Marquis shook it, she turned towards the door.

She ignored Amalita pointedly and rudely.

The Marquis put the bottle of port on a side table and hurried to escort Lady Hermione to her carriage.

When they had left the room, Amalita looked at the bottle of port curiously.

Then she became instinctively aware that there was something wrong.

She could not even explain exactly what she was now feeling even to herself.

Unmistakably she knew that Lady Hermione had an ulterior motive in giving the Marquis a gift and it was not as generous as it appeared to be on the surface.

The Marquis came back into the room.

"That was a surprise," he said. "I have never before known that woman do a generous action nor has she ever written to thank me for any hospitality she has received in this house."

He picked up the bottle of port.

"This is most certainly a rare vintage," he went on. "I do remember now that Buckworth has always been a great connoisseur of wine."

He smiled at Amalita before he added,

"I think that you and I will sample it together."

"No, *no!*" Amalita exclaimed. "You must not drink it! I know there is – something wrong – with it!"

The Marquis stared at her.

"What do you mean?"

"You may think I am – being very – foolish," Amalita exclaimed, "but I know instinctively when – something is wrong or someone is – going to be hurt. So I feel sure that if you do – drink this wine it will – in some way hurt you, even kill you."

The Marquis looked at her in sheer amazement,

Then he responded,

"I think, my dear, you are exaggerating what we might call Lady Hermione's wickedness. I have always thought her a bad woman, but I don't believe for one moment that she would be prepared to murder me."

"I am not quite so – sure," Amalita said, "so please – please don't drink that – wine. Throw it – away and just forget – it!"

"Can you really be asking me to do anything quite so extravagant and so unnecessary?" the

Marquis asked. "I don't mind telling you, this wine is so rare and so precious that I have tasted it only once before in my life!"

He laughed before he went on,

"In fact I would consider it a great sacrilege to destroy anything so unique."

"Please, I beg of you, do *not* – drink it and I promise you I am not – talking – nonsense," Amalita asserted.

She saw that the Marquis was not convinced and she added,

"Once when I was very small I was aware that my Nanny was in danger. I screamed and screamed until my father went to find her. He was just in time to prevent her from being gored by a bull that was in the field where I had been riding my pony."

Realising that the Marquis was listening, she went on,

"On another occasion one of my father's friends had borrowed a horse from him to go out hunting. As he went down the drive, I said to Papa,

"'Please, Papa, do not let him go – do not let him – ride that horse. I know it will – hurt him.'

"And what happened?" the Marquis asked.

"Papa thought that I was just being imaginative, but the man in question was thrown by the horse and – broke his – spine."

There was silence.

"You are being most persuasive," the Marquis said. "However I do find it hard to believe that Lady Hermione would stoop to anything so drastic as murder."

"What can I say to – convince you that you are in – danger?" Amalita asked him desperately.

To her surprise the Marquis rose and went out through the open French windows.

It was then she became aware that there was a man in the garden and, as the Marquis spoke to him, she saw that it was one of the gardeners, who had come to turn off the fountain at night and turn it on again in the morning.

"Good evening, Sam," the Marquis greeted him.

"'Evenin', my Lord," Sam said and touched his cap.

"I was just wondering if you have caught any mice in the traps you have set for them?" the Marquis asked.

"I ain't got a mouse, my Lord," Sam replied, "but I just looked in and sees a fat young rat and we don't want them gettin' into the house, my Lord, does we?"

"We certainly don't, Sam," the Marquis said. "And I would like you to bring the rat to me."

"Bring it to you, my Lord?" Sam asked in surprise. "I were about to drown 'e, I was, and set the trap again, 'case there's more of 'em breeding in the garden."

"Do that," the Marquis said, "but first bring the rat to me and also the bait you used to catch him."

"Right, my Lord."

Sam hurried away to a hut by the garden door leading into the Mews.

A few minutes later he came back carrying a strange wooden contraption that he had made himself.

He handed it to the Marquis and with it a paper bag.

"There be enough meat in there for at least two days, my Lord," he said.

"Thank you, Sam." The Marquis smiled. "You need not wait. I will put your trap outside the door when I go up to bed."

"Thank you, my Lord," Sam replied, "and be careful of that there rat. They bites somethin' terrible!"

"I am sure they do," the Marquis grinned.

Sam touched his cap and ambled away.

The Marquis carried the trap into the sitting room.

He put it down on one of the tables and Amalita saw it contained a large rat.

She felt herself shudder because she had always had a horror of vermin.

The Marquis opened up the paper bag and it contained the two large pieces of fresh meat. He put it down on the table and fetched a glass from the grog tray in a corner of the room.

Amalita watched him without speaking, knowing what he was going to do.

If she was mistaken in what she felt about the port, she would feel very stupid and childish.

The Marquis drew the cork from the bottle and poured a little of the port into the glass.

It was the usual dark red of vintage port and Amalita thought it looked really impossible that anyone could have tampered with it.

She was, however, still totally convinced in her own mind that there was something wrong.

The Marquis slipped a piece of the meat into the glass of port and it was very soon soaked with it apart from the corner he was holding.

Lifting it out of the glass, he put the untouched piece of meat on top of it.

The trap was made of wood and wire and there was a door, which opened at the back of it.

The rat was looking at the lit room curiously as if he thought it was new territory to explore.

Quickly the Marquis then inserted the meat through the door at the back and closed it.

Instantly the rat was aware that there was food nearby and started to turn round.

It was not easy because the trap was narrow.

However, he managed it and gulped down the meat greedily.

Now the Marquis and Amalita were watching tensely.

Neither of them moved.

Having eaten the fresh meat, the rat then sniffed at the piece beneath it.

Tentatively he took a bite as Amalita held her breath.

If he refused to go any further, the experiment would prove negative and the Marquis would tell her once again to stop being foolish.

Then he would drink the port –

The rat took another bite.

Then, as he decided that the meat despite its unusual taste was edible, he ate every scrap of it.

"He then sniffed around the floor of the trap, as if he hoped that there was some more.

Amalita knew then that the experiment had failed.

If the port was as dangerous as her instinct had told her it was, the rat would now be showing some signs of being affected by it.

Then suddenly and without any warning the rat turned over on its side.

For a second Amalita could not believe it had actually happened.

The rat did not move and she knew that it was dead. It seemed incredible that it should have happened so fast.

At that moment the door opened and the Earl came in.

Without thinking and without considering in any way what she was doing, Amalita ran to him.

She flung herself against him.

"She was – trying to kill him! She was trying to – kill him!" she cried. "How – could she do anything so – wrong and so – wicked."

Her voice broke and she hid her face against the Earl's shoulder.

He put his arm around her and said to his father,

"What is all this about? What has happened?"

The Marquis was staring at the rat as if he could not believe that the creature was really dead.

In a voice of horror he replied,

"Lady Hermione brought me a bottle of a rare vintage port as a present. I was just about to drink it when Lady Maulpin told me she was convinced that it was poisoned. It was and she has saved my life!"

The Earl could see the rat lying dead in the trap and the bottle of port standing beside it.

He understood at once what had happened.

"I cannot believe that Hermione could do anything so wicked," he said. "She must be mad! Did she come here herself and give it to you?"

"She did," his father replied. "She came to tell me that her husband's condition has deteriorated and her gift was an expression of his gratitude for the dinner party the other evening."

The Marquis was speaking in a low voice.

Then he walked towards the table where the trap was standing and picked it up.

"It would be a mistake for anybody to know that this has happened," he said. "I had better go and dispose of the evidence."

He walked out through the window into the garden.

Amalita raised her head to look up at the Earl.

"She meant to – k-kill him!" she sighed. "I knew it – but I was so – afraid he would not – believe me!"

"But he did and you saved him," the Earl commented.

He looked down at her, at her green eyes shocked and horrified at what had happened.

He could feel her whole body trembling against him.

"You saved him," he said again.

Then very gently he bent his head and his lips found hers.

For a moment, bewildered by all that had happened, Amalita did not realise that she was being kissed.

Then the pressure of the Earl's lips and the tightness of his arms as he held her against him swept away all the horror that she was feeling.

It gave her instead an ecstasy she had never known before.

It was so wonderful, so indescribable and at the same time so compelling that she pressed herself even closer to the Earl.

As he kissed her and went on kissing her, she knew, as if somebody was telling her so, that this was *love*.

She loved him and she had not realised it ever since he had come to her bedroom and she had sent him away.

The Earl drew her closer still.

Then he raised his head up and looked down into her eyes.

He was thinking that it was impossible for any woman to be so beautiful and so unbelievably attractive.

Although he could hardly believe it himself, she was a part of him.

"I love you so much, my darling," he sighed, "and I think, although you may not admit it, that you love me a little."

Then he was kissing her again, kissing her eyes, her cheeks and once more her lips.

Her whole body seemed to vibrate to him.

Thrills ran through her and she felt as if her heart was bursting with the glory of it.

She knew now that this was the love she had always longed for but thought that she would never find.

It seemed as if a century passed.

Yet it must have been a few minutes before the Earl said,

"My precious, how can you be so clever as to save my father's life."

For a moment it was really impossible for Amalita to understand what he was saying.

Then she said and the horror was back in her voice,

"She has – failed, but she may well – try again – perhaps he should – go away – perhaps he should hide."

She was trying to think coherently, but then the words seemed to come without her controlling them.

The Earl kissed her again.

Although she knew it was the most wonderful thing that had ever happened, she was still worrying about the Marquis.

When his lips were no longer touching hers, she said,

"We have to – talk – we have to think of your father and if there is a scandal – that too would – hurt him."

"I have already thought of that," the Earl replied, "and I love you, my precious one, for thinking of him."

"You must – save him – you really must!" Amalita persisted.

She thought that the Earl did not understand and she went on,

"When she – knows that she has failed – this time, she may try – something else."

"You said we must save him," the Earl said quietly, "and that is what we will do. It is quite easy if you will help me."

"Of course I – will help – you," Amalita answered.

She shivered.

"It was horrifying – petrifying – to watch the rat turn on his side and – and die! It might – have been – your father who was – lying dead."

The Earl's arms tightened.

"It is something you must forget," he said. "You and I will save my father from any further attempts on his life."

"H-how can – we do – that?" Amalita asked.

"It is quite simple," the Earl replied. "Hermione wants me to marry her, but if I am already married, she will have to accept the inevitable."

Amalita looked at him not understanding what he was saying.

Then he added gently,

"If you are my wife, my darling, you will be able to protect my father from any more murderous attempts. I will also make sure through my friends in Scotland Yard that it is something that she does not dare to try again."

Amalita could not take in what he was saying to her.

Then she looked up into his eyes.

She felt as if the whole room was suddenly filled with a dazzling light.

"Are – you really," she asked in a whisper, "asking me to – marry you?"

"I intend to marry you, my darling," the Earl replied, "and I will not take 'no' for an answer."

He pulled her a little closer as he said,

"I am not just thinking of my father but also myself. I want you, Amalita. I love you as I have never loved any woman before."

Amalita felt as if the light covering now them was too dazzling to be borne.

Then, as if a cold hand started gripping her heart, she remembered and hid her face against his shoulder.

"I do love – you," she whispered, "but – I cannot – marry you!"

The Earl kissed her hair.

"Why not, my lovely one? You know that you already belong to me."

There was silence.

Then Amalita said in a voice he could hardly hear,

"I-I have – lied to you, I am not – who you think I am."

The Earl smiled.

"I think," he said quietly, "that your name is 'Amalita' and you are the elder daughter of Sir Frederick Maulpin."

What he said was such a surprise that Amalita raised her face to look at him, her eyes wide with astonishment.

"H-how did you – know? How – did you guess?" she asked.

The Earl smiled again.

"I have been somewhat curious about you ever since you arrived," he answered. "I knew there was something about you that was not quite right."

He felt Amalita stiffen and he continued,

"Not wrong, my precious. So it is just that, like you, I have an intuition. It told me, to put it bluntly, you were not who you purported to be."

"H-how could you have – known that?"

"How could *you* have known that the port would kill my father?"

Amalita put her head back on his shoulder.

"So you did not believe that I was – Lady Maulpin?"

"Not after you had sent me away when I came to say 'goodnight'."

"I-I was – shocked," Amalita whispered.

"I knew that" he said, "and I was ashamed of myself for being such a stupid clumsy fool. I should have realised that you were very young, very innocent and, my darling Amalita, very pure."

As if she excited him, he kissed her again and they clung to each other as he went on,

"I think I am the first man who has kissed you and I swear I will be the last!"

"How – how did – you know my – name?" Amalita asked when she could speak.

"I went this afternoon after I had been playing polo," the Earl replied, "to see a very old friend of your father's, somebody who was very much in love with him and was broken-hearted when he married someone else."

"It was – clever of you to think there was – someone who knew – the truth," Amalita commented.

"She told me," he went on, "that she very occasionally heard news of Sir Frederick after he went to the country. He wrote her a letter telling her that he had a daughter who was so beautiful that he had Christened her 'Amalita' because she looked just like a Greek Goddess even at that age."

"So – that is how you knew," Amalita said. "I knew before that that you were not a married woman of twenty-six and the first thing I am going to do, my precious, is to take away the Wedding ring you are wearing on the third finger of your left hand, which I do intend to replace very quickly with my own to prove that you belong to me."

"You do – really want – me?" Amalita asked shyly.

"I will explain to you exactly how much I want you as soon as we are married," he said. "And that, my darling, because we are also protecting Papa, is going to be as soon as I can get a Special Licence. Then we will go away on our honeymoon."

"How can I – possibly marry – you when everyone – thinks I am Papa's – second – wife and – his widow?"

"That is something that we will work on together very efficiently," the Earl said confidently. "I promise you I am an expert at solving problems and conundrums that puzzle everybody else."

"I love you," Amalita said, "and I believe you could do anything, but I am a little afraid that if people discover I lied and pretended to be Carolyn's stepmother, it might hurt her in some way."

"We will save Carolyn, just as we will also save my father," the Earl answered, "and I promise that both of them will continue to be safe and protected by you and me."

"But – how – *how*?" Amalita asked.

"You must trust me," he said, "and the best way to do that is to tell me again that you love me."

"Oh – I do – love you – I *adore* – you!" Amalita said, "but I still – cannot believe – that you really love me."

"I love you until I have no words in which to express how much," the Earl replied with deep sincerity.

Then he was kissing her again, kissing her until they were no longer on earth but flying in the sky.

The future for them both could be expressed in one word.

Love.

Coming back from the bottom of the garden where he had buried the dead rat, the Marquis put the empty trap down outside the window.

Having done so, he straightened himself and looked inside the room.

To his astonishment he then saw two people clasped together in a passionate embrace.

He looked at them in amazement and then tactfully he went stealthily back into the garden.

As he walked to the fountain, he thought that this was certainly something he had not expected.

But as far as he was concerned, it could not be better.

'Good comes out of evil,' he said to himself and then chuckled.

OTHER BOOKS IN THIS SERIES

The Barbara Cartland Eternal Collection is the unique opportunity to collect all five hundred of the timeless beautiful romantic novels written by the world's most celebrated and enduring romantic author.

Named the Eternal Collection because Barbara's inspiring stories of pure love, just the same as love itself, the books will be published on the internet at the rate of four titles per month until all five hundred are available.

The Eternal Collection, classic pure romance available worldwide for all time.

1. Elizabethan Lover
2. The Little Pretender
3. A Ghost in Monte Carlo
4. A Duel of Hearts
5. The Saint and the Sinner
6. The Penniless Peer
7. The Proud Princess
8. The Dare-Devil Duke
9. Diona and a Dalmatian
10. A Shaft of Sunlight
11. Lies for Love
12. Love and Lucia
13. Love and the Loathsome Leopard
14. Beauty or Brains
15. The Temptation of Torilla
16. The Goddess and the Gaiety Girl
17. Fragrant Flower
18. Look, Listen and Love
19. The Duke and the Preacher's Daughter
20. A Kiss For The King
21. The Mysterious Maid-Servant
22. Lucky Logan Finds Love
23. The Wings of Ecstasy
24. Mission to Monte Carlo
25. Revenge of the Heart
26. The Unbreakable Spell
27. Never Laugh at Love
28. Bride to a Brigand
29. Lucifer and the Angel
30. Journey to a Star
31. Solita and the Spies
32. The Chieftain without a Heart
33. No Escape from Love
34. Dollars for the Duke
35. Pure and Untouched
36. Secrets
37. Fire in the Blood
38. Love, Lies and Marriage
39. The Ghost who fell in love

40. Hungry for Love
41. The wild cry of love
42. The blue eyed witch
43. The Punishment of a Vixen
44. The Secret of the Glen
45. Bride to The King
46. For All Eternity
47. A King in Love
48. A Marriage Made in Heaven
49. Who Can Deny Love?
50. Riding to The Moon
51. Wish for Love
52. Dancing on a Rainbow
53. Gypsy Magic
54. Love in the Clouds
55. Count the Stars
56. White Lilac
57. Too Precious to Lose
58. The Devil Defeated
59. An Angel Runs Away
60. The Duchess Disappeared
61. The Pretty Horse-breakers
62. The Prisoner of Love
63. Ola and the Sea Wolf
64. The Castle made for Love
65. A Heart is Stolen
66. The Love Pirate
67. As Eagles Fly
68. The Magic of Love
69. Love Leaves at Midnight
70. A Witch's Spell
71. Love Comes West
72. The Impetuous Duchess
73. A Tangled Web
74. Love Lifts the Curse
75. Saved By A Saint
76. Love is Dangerous
77. The Poor Governess
78. The Peril and the Prince
79. A Very Unusual Wife
80. Say Yes Samantha
81. Punished with love
82. A Royal Rebuke
83. The Husband Hunters
84. Signpost To Love
85. Love Forbidden
86. Gift of the Gods
87. The Outrageous Lady
88. The Slaves of Love
89. The Disgraceful Duke
90. The Unwanted Wedding
91. Lord Ravenscar's Revenge
92. From Hate to Love
93. A Very Naughty Angel
94. The Innocent Imposter
95. A Rebel Princess
96. A Wish Come True
97. Haunted
98. Passions In The Sand
99. Little White Doves of Love
100. A Portrait of Love
101. The Enchanted Waltz
102. Alone and Afraid
103. The Call of the Highlands
104. The Glittering Lights
105. An Angel in Hell
106. Only a Dream
107. A Nightingale Sang
108. Pride and the Poor Princess
109. Stars in my Heart
110. The Fire of Love
111. A Dream from the Night
112. Sweet Enchantress
113. The Kiss of the Devil
114. Fascination in France
115. Love Runs in
116. Lost Enchantment
117. Love is Innocent
118. The Love Trap
119. No Darkness for Love
120. Kiss from a Stranger
121. The Flame Is Love
122. A Touch Of Love

123. The Dangerous Dandy
124. In Love In Lucca
125. The Karma of Love
126. Magic from the Heart
127. Paradise Found
128. Only Love
129. A Duel with Destiny
130. The Heart of the Clan
131. The Ruthless Rake
132. Revenge Is Sweet
133. Fire on the Snow
134. A Revolution of Love
135. Love at the Helm
136. Listen to Love
137. Love Casts out Fear
138. The Devilish Deception
139. Riding in the Sky
140. The Wonderful Dream
141. This Time it's Love
142. The River of Love
143. A Gentleman in Love
144. The Island of Love
145. Miracle for a Madonna
146. The Storms of Love
147. The Prince and the Pekingese
148. The Golden Cage
149. Theresa and a Tiger
150. The Goddess of Love
151. Alone in Paris
152. The Earl Rings a Belle
153. The Runaway Heart
154. From Hell to Heaven
155. Love in the Ruins
156. Crowned with Love
157. Love is a Maze
158. Hidden by Love
159. Love Is The Key
160. A Miracle In Music
161. The Race For Love
162. Call of The Heart
163. The Curse of the Clan
164. Saved by Love
165. The Tears of Love
166. Winged Magic
167. Born of Love
168. Love Holds the Cards
169. A Chieftain Finds Love
170. The Horizons of Love
171. The Marquis Wins
172. A Duke in Danger
173. Warned by a Ghost
174. Forced to Marry
175. Sweet Adventure
176. Love is a Gamble
177. Love on the Wind
178. Looking for Love
179. Love is the Enemy
180. The Passion and the Flower
181. The Reluctant Bride
182. Safe in Paradise
183. The Temple of Love
184. Love at First Sight
185. The Scots Never Forget
186. The Golden Gondola
187. No Time for Love
188. Love in the Moon
189. A Hazard of Hearts
190. Just Fate
191. The Kiss of Paris
192. Little Tongues of Fire
193. Love under Fire
194. The Magnificent Marriage
195. Moon over Eden
196. The Dream and The Glory
197. A Victory for Love
198. A Princess in Distress
199. A Gamble with Hearts
200. Love strikes a Devil
201. In the arms of Love
202. Love in the Dark
203. Love Wins
204. The Marquis Who Hated Women
205. Love is Invincible
206. Love Climbs in
207. The Queen Saves the King
208. The Duke Comes Home

Printed in Great Britain
by Amazon